HOW I SURVIVED MIDDLE SCHOOL

Caught in the Web

Michelle

Check out these other books in the
How I Survived Middle School series by Nancy Krulik

HOW I SURVIVED MIDDLE SCHOOL

Caught in the Web

By Nancy Krulik

SCHOLASTIC INC.

New York   Toronto   London   Auckland   Sydney
Mexico City   New Delhi   Hong Kong   Buenos Aires

For Ian, who often gets caught up in the web

No part of this publication may be reproduced, stored in a retrieval system, or transmitted in any form or by any means, electronic, mechanical, photocopying, recording, or otherwise, without written permission of the publisher. For information regarding permission, write to Scholastic Inc., Attention: Permissions Department, 557 Broadway, New York, NY 10012.

ISBN-13: 978-0-545-09273-9
ISBN-10: 0-545-09273-6

Copyright © 2009 by Nancy Krulik.

12 11 10 9 8 7 6 5 4 3 2   9 10 11 12 13 14/0

Printed in the U.S.A.
First printing, April 2009

What's Your Confidence Quotient?

Are you cool and confident or shy and unsure? The first step toward figuring out where you stand is to take this quiz! Don't worry – there are no right or wrong answers. You can be completely confident that this quiz will tell you the truth.

1. **Tra la la! It's tryout time for your school's holiday concert. You've always wanted to be a singer, and this could be your chance to go from singing in the shower to showering an audience with song. How do you handle getting ready for the challenge?**

   A. Practice day and night for the chorus tryouts.
   B. You don't do anything. You know you have a great voice; you might even get a solo.
   C. You chicken out just minutes before the big audition. It's just too scary.

2. **You've studied all week for your big history test. For once, you actually finish the exam early! In fact, most of the class is still working on it. What's your next move?**

A. Drop it on the teacher's desk and go. You totally know this stuff.

B. Go over every question on the test again. If everyone else is struggling with it, you must have missed something.

C. Take a few more minutes to check over some of the tougher questions.

3. **You're in dance class when your instructor heaps some heavy praise on you for your perfect pirouette. What's your reaction?**

A. Look around to see who's dancing behind you. Maybe that's the dancer your teacher is actually speaking to.

B. You're incredibly blown away by the praise, and vow to work harder to show your teacher that your pirouette was no fluke.

C. You're not surprised at all. Of course she complimented you. Everyone knows you're the best dancer in the class.

4. **You're sitting in French class when a messenger arrives with a note asking you to go to the principal. What are you thinking as you stroll through the halls?**

A. You must have been selected to represent the school in some huge contest.

B. You have no idea what this could be about. You hope it's good news.

C. You worry that you've been turned in for getting to school late twice last week.

5. There's an amazing new short haircut you've seen in a magazine and you could really use a new haircut — it's been months since your last one. What's your next move?

A. You ask your stylist for a new look — not something as drastically different as what you saw in the magazine picture, but different just the same.

B. You ask for a trim and keep the same style you've had for a while.

C. You go for the new short 'do. It's time for a radical change. You know you're going to look great no matter what!

6. The school cutie is staring at you from across the room. What's your reaction?

A. Walk over and start chatting him up. It's no surprise he's staring at you!

B. Check your shoes to see if you're trailing toilet paper from your trip to the bathroom.

C. Smile shyly in his direction.

7. **You're at a family wedding when your little cousin begs you to dance with him. A few minutes into the dance you notice that you two are the only ones on the floor and everyone is staring at you. What now?**

A. You keep on boogying. You're glad everyone is getting a good look at your slick moves — and your new dress.

B. You keep dancing but you tone down your dance moves. You really don't want to draw more attention to yourself than need be — but you don't want to insult your little cousin, either.

C. You stop dancing immediately and leave the dance floor. This is just too embarrassing.

8. **There's a new girl in school, and your homeroom teacher assigns you the task of taking her around. She's from another state and dresses differently than the kids in your neighborhood – and not necessarily in a good way. What's your reaction to being given the job of tour guide?**

A. Beg off, saying that you aren't feeling well and might be going home early.

B. Cheerfully take on the assignment. You know that being seen with you will instantly give this girl popularity.

C. Take on the job and hope that your friends will be accepting of someone new and a little bit different.

Okay, now it's time to total up your score.

1. A) 2 points   B) 3 points   C) 1 point
2. A) 3 points   B) 1 point   C) 2 points
3. A) 1 point   B) 2 points   C) 3 points
4. A) 3 points   B) 2 points   C) 1 point
5. A) 2 points   B) 1 point   C) 3 points
6. A) 3 points   B) 1 point   C) 2 points
7. A) 3 points   B) 2 points   C) 1 point
8. A) 1 point   B) 3 points   C) 2 points

What does your score say about you?

19-24 points: Uh-oh. Sounds like someone might need to stop off at a bakery and order a slice of humble pie. Remember, there's a thin line between being confident and being just plain haughty. Try not to cross it. After all, nobody's perfect — not even you.

13-18 points: Here's a compliment you should accept gracefully: You have mastered the fine art of being confident and self-assured without coming off as conceited. Congrats!

8-12 points: You certainly are hard on yourself. It's important that you start to realize how terrific you really are. The minute you develop confidence in yourself, everyone else will, too!

Chapter
ONE

"I CAN'T BELIEVE IT," my friend Felicia groaned. "You have more than a hundred channels and there's nothing on! TV really stinks."

I pushed the button on the remote and kept searching for something Felicia, our friend Rachel, and I would all enjoy. But Felicia was right. There wasn't anything on. Just a bunch of old cartoons, news shows, baseball, and home shopping. Sunday afternoon TV can be pretty lousy. But it was raining, so we were stuck inside.

"You want to play Monopoly?" I asked my friends.

"We played that last time we were here, Jenny," Felicia reminded me. "You beat us both pretty badly."

I smiled. That was the truth. I'm a whiz at Monopoly. Donald Trump has nothing on me.

"I'm not into losing today," Felicia told me.

"Do you have any good movies?" Rachel wondered.

I shrugged. "None that the three of us haven't seen, like, a billion times," I told her.

"We've sure been friends forever," Felicia said with a laugh. "Sometimes I feel like there's nothing we haven't done or seen together."

That was the truth. Rachel, Felicia, and I had been

friends since kindergarten, and now we were in sixth grade. That meant we'd gone through almost seven years of birthday parties, sleepovers, chicken pox, phone conversations, and Rachel's bad jokes together.

"I always love being at your house, Jenny," Felicia said. "Even on rainy days. Remember that time in third grade when it rained on Easter and your folks had their Easter egg hunt *inside*?"

"I was the one who found the egg that was hidden in the toilet paper roll!" Rachel exclaimed proudly.

"Only because you had to go to the bathroom right in the middle of the whole thing," Felicia reminded her.

"Yeah, but Rachel won the chocolate bunny, anyway," I said. "My dad gave it to the person who found the egg that was hidden in the hardest place."

"Those were good times." Rachel smiled, remembering. "That chocolate bunny was delicious."

"I think we have that Easter egg hunt on tape somewhere," I said. "My mom's big on filming stuff like that. She's kind of like Marc that way."

Rachel and Felicia nodded. They knew what I meant. Our friend Marc doesn't go anywhere without his digital camcorder. He wants to be a movie director one day, so he spends a lot of time practicing.

"You guys want to watch the tape?" I asked them.

"Totally!" Rachel exclaimed.

"I love home movies," Felicia added.

"Speaking of movies, did you guys hear the one about

the woman who brought her dog to a movie theater?" Rachel asked Felicia and me with a grin. We both shook our heads, so Rachel continued her joke. "After the film was over, a man stopped her and said, 'I was amazed at your dog. He really seemed to like the movie. He cried at the right times, and laughed at the right times. He even yawned when it got kind of boring. Don't you think that's unusual?' The woman nodded. 'Very unusual,' she told the man. 'Especially since he hated the book.'"

Rachel began to laugh. Felicia and I laughed, too, which was actually pretty unusual, since Rachel's jokes are usually awful. Rachel was obviously encouraged by our laughter because she grinned and said, "If you liked that one, you'll *love* this one. Why did the movie star —"

"Whoa! Why not quit while you're ahead?" Felicia said, stopping Rachel before she could ruin the moment by telling another joke. "Jen, go get the tape."

"Right away," I said with a giggle. I knew Rachel wasn't insulted by Felicia's teasing. She knew it was all in fun. Besides, even *she* admitted that not all of her jokes were great.

"Here it is!" I exclaimed as I pulled the tape from a box of assorted home movies. I read the label. "'Easter Egg Hunt. Jenny, age nine.'"

"That's the one," Rachel said.

"I can't believe you still have a VCR," Felicia said. "We only have a DVD player at my house."

"My folks kept the VCR so we could keep on playing

our old home movies," I explained. "But I think my dad's going to get the tapes transferred onto DVD eventually. Everything my mom films now is on her digital camcorder, anyway." I hit the play button, and a moment later there we were (or at least there were the third grade versions of us!).

"Oh, look at you, Felicia!" Rachel said. "Nice red corduroy pants."

Felicia cringed. "Oh, man, what was I thinking?"

"Probably the same thing I was thinking when I put on that pink furry vest," I told her, as I checked out my image on the screen.

"Look at how I'm jumping around with that egg in my hand," Rachel groaned. "This goes no further than this room, okay, you guys?"

Felicia and I nodded in agreement.

"Look at you, Jenny! You have a chocolate mustache," Felicia giggled, pointing to the TV.

"I ate a lot of chocolate that day," I admitted. "We all did. Look at how we're bouncing around the room. We all had major sugar rushes!"

Just then, the image of a small girl with long blond curls flashed onto the screen. She twirled around like a ballerina and then ran over to give me a big hug.

Felicia, Rachel, and I stopped giggling. The sight of Addie Wilson in the home movies made us all uncomfortable.

I watched as the third grade Addie on the screen took

the third grade me by the hand and led me around the room. A moment later we were both dancing some bizarre ballet. Well, what *I* was doing was bizarre. Addie had always been a much better dancer than I was. She still is.

It was really weird watching Addie and I getting along and acting like BFFs on the tape, because that's definitely not the way we are now. As close as she and I were back in third grade is exactly how far apart we are now that we're in middle school.

Back in third grade I'd expected to be Addie's BFF forever (which is what that second F stands for, after all). But apparently Addie had different plans, because when I went away to camp last summer, she found a new group of friends. And I wasn't part of that crowd.

It's not that I didn't make an effort to be part of Addie's middle school life. When I first started middle school, I tried everything to get along with Addie's new friends. I wore the same clothes they did, and I listened to the same music. I even tried to sit at their lunch table. But they wouldn't make room for me. They just didn't want me around at all. The Pops are a very exclusive group.

The Pops. That's what my friends and I call Addie and her friends. Pop as in *pop*ular. The Pops aren't actually popular by the dictionary definition, because that would mean they have more friends than anyone else in the school. And actually, they're a really small group of friends. In middle school, the word popular has a different definition. It means being a part of the crowd everyone else wishes they could be in.

I think every school has its own group of Pops. They're the ones who wear the coolest clothes, have the best makeup, and only hang out with each other. Basically, they're at the top of the middle school food chain. That was where Addie was right now. And despite the fact that she and I had been inseparable all through elementary school, she hadn't made any effort at all to include me in her middle school Pop world.

Of course, that didn't mean I was friendless. Besides Rachel and Felicia, I had plenty of cool friends. But we weren't Pops, and we knew it. And despite the fact that we all had a blast together, I had a feeling most of us were at least curious about what it would feel like to be a Pop.

"Okay, enough of this," Rachel said, standing up. "It's becoming The Addie Wilson Show. Besides, now I'm hungry. Do you have any chocolate?"

I nodded. "Lots." I thought for a minute. "Hey, my mom's in the kitchen. Maybe she'll let us make a chocolate fondue."

"Mmmm," Felicia said. "That sounds really good."

I got the idea for chocolate fondue from my favorite website, middleschoolsurvival.com. It's this really cool site that has all sorts of quizzes, tips, and ideas for getting through middle school. My friends and I practically live by it.

I'm only allowed to make chocolate fondue if my mom or dad are around, because it involves using the stove. "Hey, Mom, can we make a chocolate fondue?" I asked, as I ran into the kitchen with Rachel and Felicia trailing close behind.

"I don't see why not," my mom replied. "We have plenty of fruit, and I think there are big marshmallows left in the cupboard."

"Mrs. McAfee, you're the best," Rachel told my mom.

My mother laughed. "I try," she replied with a grin.

"I'll print out a copy of the recipe!" I shouted as I raced over to the computer and typed in www.middleschool survival.com. A minute later, I had the directions for making fondue in my hand.

Chocolate Fondue for You

Here's a fruity treat that's sure to satisfy any chocolate lover!

YOU WILL NEED:

1 11-½ ounce package of milk chocolate chips

¼ cup milk

1 tablespoon chunky peanut butter

Assorted fruit (strawberries, apple slices, banana chunks, orange slices)

Marshmallows

Skewers

HERE'S WHAT YOU DO:

1. Combine the chocolate and milk. Stir over low heat until the chocolate is melted.
2. Stir in the peanut butter.
3. Heat until the whole mixture is warm and melted.
4. Place the fruit and marshmallows on skewers.
5. Dip the fruit and marshmallows in the chocolate–milk–peanut butter mixture and dig in!

Soon we were happily scarfing down fruit and marshmallows covered in chocolate and peanut butter. A year ago, Addie would have been right there with us, probably singing some weird song about chocolate-covered strawberries or making up a fun fondue dance. But that was the old Addie. The new *Pop* Addie was way too cool to dance and sing for no reason. She was also too cool to hang out with Rachel, Felicia, or me. Things change.

"Stay right there. I just have to film you while you eat fondue," my mother said, hurrying to the hall closet to get the digital video camera.

"Oh, Mom," I groaned. But I knew there was no stopping her. My mom documents everything at our house with home movies. Someday, Felicia, Rachel, and I would be watching our chocolate fondue day on TV, just like we'd watched the old tape of the Easter egg hunt today. Some things *never* change.

Chapter
TWO

"I THINK I DID pretty well on that English test this morning," my friend Chloe said as we sat down together in the school cafeteria the next day. "Of course, I had plenty of time to study with all that rain yesterday. There was nothing else to do."

"The weather was really grotty," our friend Samantha agreed in her sophisticated British accent. "I felt like I was back in London."

"Is the TV as bad in London as it is here?" I asked her. "Felicia, Rachel, and I were looking for something to watch all afternoon. There was nothing on."

"That's because you were watching regular TV shows," our friend Marc pointed out to me.

"Is there another kind of show?" I asked him.

"Well, sort of," he said. "I found one or two webcasts on the computer that were interesting."

"What's a webcast?" I asked.

"It's a show, but it's broadcast live on the Internet," Marc explained.

"I've seen one or two of those," our friend Josh said. "Bill Gates has done a lot of them. I watched one once where he was talking about the future of the Internet."

I smiled. I could see why watching a computer genius like Bill Gates talking about the Internet would interest Josh. After all, he was pretty much a genius himself.

"I was actually watching a webcast that a couple of high school kids did in their basement," Marc said. "They were playing musical instruments. They were really bad, but that's what made it funny."

Personally, I didn't think watching high school kids play instruments badly on a computer sounded any better than watching the home shopping channel, but everyone else seemed intrigued by the webcast idea.

"I wonder if it's hard to do a webcast," Chloe mused.

"Uh-oh . . ." Sam said. "I know what's coming now."

"What?" Chloe asked, trying to sound innocent, but not succeeding.

"You've just discovered a new way to make yourself famous," Sam told her.

Chloe shrugged. "I'm nothing if not ambitious," she admitted. Then she turned back to Marc. "Can anyone do a webcast? Or do you have to have writers, producers, and directors like on regular TV?"

"Anyone can do one," Marc said. "That's the cool thing about the Internet. It's open to everyone. And it's not that hard either. All you need is —"

"Aaaachooooooo!"

Marc's explanation of how to make a webcast was interrupted by a loud sneeze from my friend Carolyn. She was walking toward our table along with her twin sister, Marilyn, and another seventh grader, our pal Liza.

"Bless you," Marilyn said to her sister.

"Thanks," Carolyn answered. Only it sounded more like "Danks," because her nose was all stuffed up.

"Aaaachooooo!" Carolyn sneezed again, only louder this time. In fact, she sneezed so hard she shook her lunch tray and spilled some of her fruit juice.

"Bless you," Marilyn repeated.

"Danks," Carolyn said again. Then she looked down. "Oh, man, I just spilled this red stuff on my shirt."

"It'll come out," Marilyn assured her.

"Hurry to the bathroom and rinse it with water before it stains," Liza suggested.

"Oh, no," Marilyn began. "We can't . . ."

". . . go in there." Carolyn finished.

I knew exactly why the twins didn't want to go into the bathroom. The girls' room near the cafeteria was Pop territory. They used it as their own personal clubhouse during lunch. And they made it very uncomfortable for any non-Pop who wandered in there. I wasn't exactly sure what the Pops did in there every day, although I suspected it had something to do with making fun of other people.

"Aaachoo!" Carolyn sneezed again, harder this time.

"Oooh, stay away from them," Dana Harrison said to her friend Claire as they and the other Pops passed by our table. "You might catch something."

"Something like eternal geekiness," Claire said, in a voice that was loud enough for us to hear. All the other Pops began to laugh hysterically. Carolyn sighed and looked down at the ground.

I was amazed at just how rude the Pops could be. But I wasn't surprised by their behavior. They always talked like that. The Pops didn't need to be in their girls' room clubhouse to make fun of people. They did that anywhere they wanted to. The bathroom was just convenient because it had mirrors, and the Pops needed those to help them touch up their makeup.

"Anyway, what were we talking about before we were so rudely interrupted?" Chloe asked as the Pops moved on.

By the way she said it, I could tell she definitely remembered what our conversation had been about.

"Oh, yeah, webcast shows," Chloe said, pretending to suddenly recall the topic. "Wouldn't it be so cool if we could do one?"

"*We*?" Marc asked. "You don't know anything about doing a webcast. I only learned how to do it from being in the film club. We do live broadcasts of a lot of sporting events, so I've seen how it works."

"That's why you would be the director," Chloe told him.

Marc smiled. He seemed very pleased with that title, seeing as that's what he wants to be when he grows up. I had to hand it to Chloe. Sometimes she knew exactly what to say to get what she wanted.

"And Liza, you could design the sets," Chloe continued, "just like you did for the school play. Those were amazing."

Now *Liza* was the one beaming. And she had a right to be. The sets she'd built for our school's production of *You're a Good Man, Charlie Brown* had been incredible.

"It *is* fun to build sets," Liza agreed.

"So if I'm doing the directing, and Liza's making the sets, what will you be doing?" Marc asked, as if he didn't already know.

"I'll be the on-air talent," Chloe said. She looked around the table at the rest of us. "I read in a magazine that's what they call the performers."

"What kind of show can you do . . ." Marilyn began.

". . . all by yourself?" Carolyn finished.

"I could sing and dance," Chloe said.

Sam frowned slightly. "No offense," she said gently, "but people want variety in their shows. Watching just one person could get sort of dull."

"Are you saying I'm boring?" Chloe demanded. Obviously she *had* taken offense to what Sam had said.

"Don't get upset," Sam replied. "You're not boring. But people like to see a lot of different kinds of talent."

"We could have a variety show," Josh said. "Like a weekly talent show. They were huge in the fifties and sixties."

We all stared at him with surprise.

"What?" Josh asked. "I can't know anything about pop culture?"

"Well, what kinds of other acts can we have?" Chloe asked. She sounded slightly less enthusiastic.

"I think between all of us we can come up with a few talents," I said. "None as amazing as your singing, but good ones." I added that last part to make her feel better. It seemed to work, because she smiled.

"Maybe we should meet after school today to plan," Chloe suggested. She turned to Marc. "Are you into doing this?"

"Definitely," he said. "It's good practice for when I start directing the real thing."

"We have to make *this* the real thing," Chloe said. "We'll do it professionally. In fact, today we should meet in our actual studio."

"What studio?" Marc asked her.

"We can use my basement," Chloe told him. "It's perfect. No one ever goes down there. You can use a laptop for a webcast, can't you?"

Marc nodded. "Of course. As long as you have access to the Internet down there."

"We have Wi-Fi in the whole house," Chloe told him.

"Then it'll work," Marc assured her. "I'll bring my laptop over. It's brand new. Totally state of the art."

"Perfect!" Chloe was getting so excited that she was starting to actually bounce up and down in her chair. "So who can meet in our *studio* right after school?"

"I can," I said. "I don't have anything after school."

"I can come over, too," Liza said. "But only for an hour. Then I have to meet with my tutor."

"Aaachoo!" Carolyn sneezed. "We can come . . ."

". . . for a little while," Marilyn said. Then she turned to her sister. "Gesundheit."

"Danks," Carolyn said.

"I have tae kwon do," Josh said. "So I have to miss the meeting. And I think Felicia has a sports club meeting at the community center."

"Funny how you know her schedule," Sam teased him.

Josh blushed, but he didn't say anything. We all know that Josh and Felicia are boyfriend and girlfriend, and Josh knows we know. But he still gets embarrassed when we talk about it.

"If Felicia has sports club, then Rachel must, too," Chloe said. "But we can call them later and ask them if they want to be part of the webcast." She turned to Sam. "How about you?"

Sam frowned. "I have to go right home after school pretty much every day from now on," she said.

"Are you grounded?" Marc asked her.

Sam shook her head. "No. My mum says I can go out whenever I want . . . as long as I do what she wants me to do. And I don't want to do that."

"What does your mom want you to do?" Carolyn and Marilyn both asked at the exact same time.

I giggled. "I love the way you guys do that."

"It's a twin thing," they said together. Then they turned their attention back to Sam.

"It's no big deal," she told us quietly. "Mum will get over it soon, I'm sure."

I could tell Sam didn't want to talk about whatever argument she was having with her mother, so I changed the subject. "Do you want to go to a different bathroom to wash the juice off of your shirt?" I asked Carolyn.

"I'll go with you," Marilyn told Carolyn. "I have an extra shirt in my locker you can change into. I think it's yours anyway."

"Danks," Carolyn said, sounding even more stuffed up than before. "I don't want to walk around with this gross juice stain all day."

As the twins walked off together, I marveled at just how alike they were. They didn't just look alike. They walked alike and they talked alike. They even thought alike. Like two parts of a whole.

"It must be so cool to be them," I said.

"Seriously," Liza agreed. "Like having a walking, talking reflection."

"I don't think the world could take two of me," Chloe joked.

We all began to laugh. "You got that one right," Sam agreed. "They broke the mold when you were born."

"Yep, I'm one of a kind," Chloe said proudly. "Definitely."

THREE

CHLOE'S BASEMENT DIDN'T look like any TV studio I'd ever seen. (Okay, I hadn't actually seen any real TV studios, but my guess was they didn't have a washer and dryer in one corner and boxes of old clothes stacked up in another.) Still, we all fit comfortably down there, and Liza was already figuring out ways to create a stage area near the stairs.

"We could use a bedsheet as a curtain to hide the steps," she told us. "I'll decorate it with all sorts of designs. Kind of graffiti-like. That will look really cool and colorful on camera."

I stared at Liza in amazement. All I could see was a dingy basement, and she was already picturing a whole set that would transform the room completely. And the way she described it, the rest of us were beginning to see it, too.

"We're going to need a lot of lighting to get the picture right," Marc said, sounding a lot like a real director. "It's really dark down here."

"We're not going to need any lights or curtains if we don't have a show," Chloe pointed out. "I think we should plan out what I'm going to do . . ." she stopped herself. "I mean, what *we're* going to do on the first episode."

Carolyn and Marilyn looked at each other. "We know how to do this really funny mirror thing," Carolyn began.

"Our mom taught it to us when we were kids," Marilyn finished.

The twins stood up and faced each other. They stood absolutely still, staring straight ahead.

"One . . . two . . . three . . ." they counted at the exact same time, in what sounded almost like the exact same voice.

Then they began to move in perfect unison. When Marilyn raised her arm, Carolyn did, too. When Carolyn nodded her head, Marilyn did the same thing. Then Marilyn turned around slowly. Carolyn turned at the exact same time, but in the opposite direction. If they had been wearing the same clothes it really would have seemed that Marilyn was looking at herself in the mirror. Or that Carolyn was looking at *herself* in the mirror. Either way. That was the whole point.

We all watched in amazement as the twins continued their mirror trick. Carolyn smiled broadly. Marilyn smiled back at her. Then Marilyn waved. Carolyn waved. Marilyn jumped up. Carolyn jumped up. Marilyn flicked her hair behind her shoulder. And Carolyn . . .

"Aaachooo!" Carolyn sneezed.

"You ruined it!" Marilyn shouted at her sister.

"I'm sorry," Carolyn apologized. "I just have this cold. Besides, we were almost finished."

"And we got the idea," I assured her. "You guys were great! You should definitely do that on the show."

Just then, Chloe's dog, Bingo, came padding down the stairs. He looked around at all of us and began barking.

"I think Bingo wants to be in the show," I joked.

"Maybe you could do an animal act with him, Chloe," Liza suggested. "You know, like, demonstrate all the tricks he knows."

Chloe shook her head. "I'm going to sing and dance."

I had a feeling Chloe said that because Bingo didn't know that many tricks. At least, she'd never mentioned him knowing any. And believe me, if Chloe had taught her dog to roll over or play dead, she would have said something. She tells us everything.

A moment later, Bingo got bored with barking at us. He walked off and busied himself by sniffing around all of our book bags and coats, which were in a pile in the corner. I guess nothing in there smelled too interesting because a few minutes later he was sniffing around the washing machine. Finally, he trotted back upstairs.

Chloe looked down at the notebook on her lap. "Okay, so we have me singing and dancing and Marilyn and Carolyn doing their mirror act. That's not much of a show."

"Maybe Josh can do a tae kwon do demonstration," Liza suggested. "He could break a board with his foot or something."

"Does he know how to do that?" Chloe wondered.

I nodded. "Felicia told me he had to do it to get his black belt."

"Cool," Chloe said. "We'll ask him about it tomorrow. And maybe Felicia and Rachel can come up with something to do. How about you, Jenny?"

I frowned. I didn't really have any major talents. I don't dance or sing, and my only after-school activity is student council. I'm the sixth grade class president. But that meant I knew a lot about what was going on around school before other people did. Maybe there was something in that. "I could do a short newsbreak or something. I could announce what's going on at our school, and what activities the student council has planned. I figure most of the kids who will be watching will be other people from Joyce Kilmer Middle School, anyway."

"Maybe in the beginning," Chloe told me. "But once word gets out about our amazing show, people from all over will watch."

"Well, I'll worry about that when it happens," I replied. "I can always do a different kind of newscast if we attract a bigger audience."

"Jenny's right," Liza said. "Let's get the first show done, and then worry about doing more."

Marilyn nodded in agreement. Carolyn sneezed.

"We can't keep calling it *the show*," Marc pointed out. "We have to give it a name. Something really cool and catchy."

"How about *Chloe's Cool and Catchy Variety Show*?" Chloe suggested.

"Why should your name go in there?" Marc asked her.

"Well, it was sort of my idea," she replied.

Marc shook his head. "I'm the one who brought up the whole webcast thing during lunch, and I'm not asking to have *my* name in the title."

I could see Chloe was getting a little mad. So was Marc. They were really close friends, but the two of them argued all the time.

"Underground," Liza murmured suddenly.

"What?" I asked her.

"Underground," she repeated, sounding a little more sure of herself. "We should call the show *Webcast Underground*, because our studio is in the basement."

"*Webcast Underground*," Marc repeated. "I like that."

"Me, too," Marilyn said.

"I like it, too," Carolyn agreed. "Aachoo!"

"You don't sound so good," I told Carolyn. "Maybe you should go home."

"I have to get going, too," Liza said.

"Let's just decide this before we go," Marc suggested. "All in favor of calling the show *Webcast Underground*, raise your hands."

Marc, Liza, Marilyn, Carolyn, and I all raised our hands. Chloe was the only one who didn't.

"Majority rules," Marc said, as he stood up. "*Webcast Underground* it is."

"Good, I'm glad that's settled," Liza said. "Now I've really got to run."

"Me, too," I agreed. I walked over to where our stuff was piled up and picked up my book bag. "That's weird," I said.

"What is?" Marc asked me.

"I was sure I had my purple pen with the feathers on it in the front pocket of my backpack. But it's not here now."

"Maybe you left it in school," Liza said.

"I don't think so," I replied. "I just hope it didn't fall out somewhere. I always forget to zip that pocket."

"I'm sure it's in your locker," Liza assured me.

I hoped she was right. I really liked my purple feather pen.

I wasn't in my house five minutes when my cell phone began to ring. It was Chloe.

"Hey, Chlo, what's up?" I greeted her.

"I talked to Rachel, and she's in," she replied.

"Already?" I was surprised.

"Yeah, well, I really wanted to get going on this," Chloe explained. "Rachel's definitely going to do something for the show. Felicia wasn't picking up her cell, so I'll have to check with her later."

"What about Sam?" I asked.

"I called her, but apparently she and her mom are still arguing," Chloe told me. "I could hear her mom in the background telling her she had to get off the phone to practice."

"Practice what?" I wondered.

"I have no idea," she said. "But I told her we could talk in school tomorrow. I didn't want to get her in any more trouble."

"Smart move," I agreed. "So we're ready to get going on *Webcast Underground*."

Chloe was quiet for a minute. "Yeah, about that name . . ." she said finally, letting her voice drift off.

"We voted on it, Chloe," I reminded her.

"But no one is going to know what it means except us," Chloe insisted. "And I've been doing some research on the Internet. All of those old-school variety shows Josh was talking about had somebody's name in the title. There was *The Carol Burnett Show*, *Donny & Marie*, *The Sonny & Cher Show* . . ."

"I don't know who any of those people are," I told her.

"Me, neither," Chloe agreed. "But people back then must have, because those shows were really popular."

I thought for a minute. "They were probably big stars, Chloe. That's why their names were in the title."

"Maybe," Chloe said. "But I'm kind of like a star — at least at Joyce Kilmer Middle School. I was Lucy in our school play, remember?"

How could I forget? Chloe had been the understudy for that part. At the last minute the actress playing Lucy got sick, and Chloe had to perform in her place. It had almost been a complete disaster because Chloe had never learned the lines. But with the help of our whole group of friends, she'd pulled it off in the end.

"It's not really the same thing," I told Chloe gently.

"But I came up with the webcast idea," Chloe insisted.

I sighed. "We voted," I told her again quietly.

"But . . ." she began.

"Come on, Chloe, don't act so spoiled," I told her.

"I AM NOT SPOILED!" Chloe screamed into the phone.

Whoa! I'd sure struck a nerve there. "Hey, don't yell at me," I told her. "You don't have to get angry just because you're not getting your way."

Chloe took a deep breath. "Sorry," she said. "It's just that I don't think I'm spoiled. I fight for what I think is right."

"Or what you *want*," I suggested. "Because *Webcast Underground* is definitely the *right* title for the show."

"I'm not spoiled and I can prove it," Chloe insisted. "Are you near a computer now?"

"Yeah," I replied.

"Good, because my mom is using ours," Chloe explained. "Go on middleschoolsurvival.com right now and find a quiz that can tell me if I'm spoiled or not. I'll take it now and prove how not spoiled I am."

"Deal," I said, walking over to the computer and

logging on to my favorite site. A second later I'd found the perfect quiz.

Spoiler Alert

Is your Christmas wish list so long you have to write it on a roll of wrapping paper? Do you need an extra room in your home, just to house your shoes? Are you a pampered princess who gets everything she wants . . . whenever she wants it? In other words, are you spoiled rotten? Take this quiz to find out!

1. What chores do you do around the house?

A. I clean my room when my mom reminds me to.

B. I don't do chores. They would cut into my free time.

C. I clear the table, wash the dishes, take out the trash, and fold the laundry.

"That's easy," Chloe said. "I always clean my room, even without my mom asking me. But I don't do the dishes or fold laundry. I guess my answer is A."

"Cool," I said, clicking the mouse over the letter A. "Here's the next one."

2. Wow! You just won a contest. Now you have a check for one million dollars! What are you going to buy?

A. A home entertainment system for my bedroom.

B. A mansion in Bel Air.

C. The dress I saw in the window of my favorite boutique in the mall.

"Bel Air's in California, right?" Chloe asked me.

"Yep," I replied.

"Well, if I'm going to be an actress, I'm going to have to live in California," Chloe thought out loud. "Of course, I'll need a car if I live in California. And some nice clothes. Boy, this is a hard question."

"You can only choose one answer, Chlo," I reminded her.

"I know, I know," Chloe replied. "Well, if I get famous enough I can go to all sorts of movie premieres at theaters for free, and designers will send me fancy dresses to wear at all of my appearances. So I guess my biggest dream would be the mansion."

"B it is," I said as I clicked the mouse. A moment later the next question flashed on the screen.

3. It's vacation time. How does your family choose where to go?

A. We decide together.

B. My parents go where I want to go. They know it won't be a good vacation if I'm miserable.

C. I go where my parents decide to go, or I stay home with my grandparents.

"We've actually been talking about that," Chloe said. "My dad just started his new job, so he doesn't get any vacation time for a whole year. But my mom and I are thinking about doing something together. It's kind of tough because she wants to go to a place where we can sightsee and visit museums, but I just want to lie on a beach."

"Do you think you'll get your way?" I asked.

"Probably," Chloe said. "My mom doesn't mind the beach, and I would rather die than go to museums all the time."

"So should I click B?" I asked her.

"Yeah, I guess," Chloe agreed.

4. How do you feel about hand-me-downs?

A. I'll wear them if they're something I like.

B. I have no problem handing my clothes down, but I would never wear someone else's clothes.

C. Almost my entire wardrobe is made up of hand-me-downs.

"A, I guess," Chloe said. "I wear some of the stuff I get from my cousins, but most of it I really hate. They have no sense of humor."

I laughed. I knew exactly what Chloe meant. She had a great sense of humor, and her clothes reflected it. Like the T-shirt she had on today. It had said *I Do All My Own Stunts.* Just thinking about it made me laugh.

"A it is," I said, clicking the mouse. The next question popped up.

5. Whose computer are you taking this quiz on?

A. It's a family computer.

B. My own, I got it for my birthday.

C. My best friend's computer — I don't have one at home.

"Well, this is your computer, so I guess it should be C," Chloe said.

"You're the boss," I said as I clicked on C.

A moment later a new page appeared on the screen. Chloe's quiz results had been tabulated.

You answered: 2 A'S, 2 B'S, and 1 C.
So what do your answers mean?

Mostly A's: You're a perfectly normal, not-too-spoiled, kid. Sure, you like the finer things once in a while, but you don't demand them.

Mostly B's: P.U.! Something smells spoiled, and it's you! You get everything you want, but you're still not satisfied. Try stepping back and doing something for someone else once in a while. You might find it more rewarding than a fancy dress or designer shoes.

Mostly C's: You really have it rough. It's nice to give to others, but it's also okay to ask for something for yourself once in a while.

"It was a tie between being really spoiled and being totally normal," I told Chloe.

"Yeah, but I also had one C," Chloe reminded me. "And that kind of pulls me more into the not-too-spoiled category, doesn't it?"

"I guess," I agreed.

"See?" Chloe replied triumphantly. "I told you I wasn't spoiled. I'm totally normal."

"Let's not go crazy," I teased her.

Chloe giggled. "Okay, not normal. But at least in terms of being spoiled, anyway."

"So if you're not spoiled, why are you insisting on having your way about the name of our webcast?" I asked her. "Isn't the most important thing that people will be able to hear you sing and watch you dance?"

"I guess," Chloe admitted. "And anyway, if I get to be really famous, we can always change the title to *Chloe's Underground*."

I sighed. Chloe was never going to change. Which was actually okay by me. I liked her the way she was, even if she drove me crazy sometimes.

Just then, I heard barking coming from the other end of the phone. "Bingo wants to go out," Chloe told me. "Or he wants to eat. Or maybe just play. I haven't figured it out exactly yet."

"You will," I assured her. "You haven't had him that long. You only adopted him from the shelter a few months ago."

"I know," Chloe said. "But it sure would be easier if he just talked."

"That would be incredible," I replied.

"Really incredible," Chloe agreed. "Incredible enough to be on *Webcast Underground*!"

Chapter
FOUR

"OKAY, SO NOW WE'RE ALL agreed we're going to perform our first webcast on Friday," Chloe said at lunch the next afternoon.

I nodded. "I talked to Felicia and Rachel, and that day works for them also," I told the others.

"Great!" Chloe exclaimed. "Because I made these fliers to hand out." She held up a stack of yellow, red, and blue sheets of paper. "I made them the minute Marc told me what our official URL was. See, it's right there at the top of the page."

Sure enough, at the top of each flier was our official webcast URL address. And beneath it, Chloe had written:

WEBCAST UNDERGROUND

A really cool variety talent show coming to you live, right on your computer!
Featuring your favorite Joyce Kilmer Middle School stars!
Friday night at 8:00 P.M.

"'Your favorite Joyce Kilmer Middle School stars'?" Liza asked doubtfully.

"Well, I starred in the school play," Chloe pointed out. "And we're all each others' favorite people. So I'm not lying."

Liza giggled. "I guess not," she agreed.

Chloe smiled triumphantly. "So, are you going to be able to be part of the webcast on Friday?"

Sam shook her head. "I can't guarantee it, so don't count on me."

"Still fighting with your mom?" Chloe asked her.

I gasped slightly. Yesterday I had gotten the feeling that Sam didn't want to talk about what was going on with her and her mom. Obviously Chloe hadn't picked up on that.

Sam shrugged. "I just don't want to do everything she says anymore. I'm not a baby!"

We all nodded in agreement. Everyone I know has felt that way sometimes. It's something about being in middle school. Here we're expected to be responsible for ourselves. We don't get constant reminders about projects and stuff. Like, for instance, right now I was working on a project for English class. I was supposed to choose a book from the library, read it, and then come up with a game based on the characters in the book. We had three weeks to do it. Ms. Jaffe had assigned it a week ago, and that was it. She wasn't constantly reminding us to work on it or anything. We had to keep up with things on our own. "Like responsible young adults," she'd told us.

But at home we aren't treated like responsible young adults. A lot of the time our parents still treat us like little kids. It can get confusing.

Still, lately I'd been figuring out that I could get my parents to treat me more like my teachers did if I did more stuff around the house, like taking out the trash without being asked and making my bed before I left for school in the morning. The other night I even washed my own laundry (okay, with a little help from my mom, but still . . .). After I did that, my mom let me stay up late on a school night to watch the end of a movie that I had become totally hooked on. That had made me feel very grown up.

Thinking about that experience caused me to add another rule to my constantly growing list of rules about middle school that you will never find in any official school handbook.

MIDDLE SCHOOL RULE #31:

JUST BECAUSE PEOPLE CALL YOU A "YOUNG ADULT" DOESN'T MEAN THAT THEY'RE GOING TO TREAT YOU THAT WAY. IF YOU WANT GROWN-UPS TO TREAT YOU LIKE AN ADULT, YOU HAVE TO TAKE ON MORE RESPONSIBILITIES. THE MORE YOU DO THAT, THE MORE PRIVILEGES YOU'LL GET.

I didn't mention my new rule at the lunch table, though. Sam didn't seem like she was in the mood to hear anything like that. Besides, I really didn't know exactly what it was her mom wanted her to do. And she wasn't saying.

"Anyway, I might be allowed to come to your house on Friday, but then again I might not," Sam explained to Chloe. "And I don't want to mess things up for you lot. So if I can come, I'll just be a gofer."

"A what?" Liza asked her.

"A gofer," Sam said. "You know, *go for* this and *go for* that. I could run errands on the set. I heard that word on American TV. I thought it was a term you used."

I shook my head. "I've never heard it before," I admitted. "But I like it."

"Me, too," Liza said with a laugh. "Thanks for the lesson in American English."

Marc pulled out a notebook. "I'm trying to get the timings down," he said. "Chloe, your song is just over three minutes, right?"

Chloe nodded.

"And Jenny, you're talking for one minute about school events?" Marc asked.

"Yeah. It's my one minute newsbreak," I told him.

"And my tae kwon do demonstration is really quick," Josh said. "It doesn't take long to perform one form and break a few boards."

"How much time does the twins' mirror act take?" Marc asked.

Chloe looked up. "Ask them. Here they come now. I see Marilyn."

In fact, we all saw Marilyn. But none of us saw Carolyn. Ordinarily, that wouldn't have been all that odd. After all, she could have gotten stuck talking to a teacher in her last class. That had happened before. But today Marilyn was acting really strangely. She looked like she was lost. Her eyes were darting all around the cafeteria, as though she was looking for us. That was definitely weird since my friends and I sit at the exact same table every day.

"Oh, man," Liza said. "She's been like this all morning. I'll go get her."

Liza jumped up from her seat and raced over to Marilyn. The minute Marilyn spotted her, she smiled broadly, like a lost skier who'd just seen the rescue squad.

"Hi, Marilyn," I said, as she and Liza came back to our table and took their seats. I wondered if she noticed how curiously we were all looking at her.

"Hi," Marilyn replied in a slightly dazed voice.

"Where's Carolyn?" Chloe asked her.

"Home . . ." Marilyn's voice drifted off for a minute. Then she added, "Sick."

"What's wrong with her?" Sam asked her.

"Flu," Marilyn told her. "The doctor . . ." Marilyn's voice drifted off again. Then, after realizing that Carolyn wasn't there to finish her thought, she continued, "The doctor says she's going to have to be in bed at least until the weekend."

"The *weekend*!" Chloe exclaimed. She sounded really upset.

"Relax, Chloe," Sam said. "It's just the flu, not some life-threatening illness."

"Carolyn will be fine," Liza assured her.

"Oh, yeah, I'm sure," Chloe said. "But the twins' act won't be."

We all just stared at her. Our friend was sick, and all she could think about was the webcast!

"What?" Chloe demanded. "Somebody has to stay on top of things. It takes a lot of work to put a show like ours together."

"I thought that was my job as the director," Marc pointed out.

"Well, I figured you'd need some help," Chloe replied.

"I'm doing fine," Marc assured her. "You work on your song. I'll work on getting a replacement act for the mirror thing. Is there something you can do on your own, Marilyn?"

I looked over at Marilyn. It sure didn't seem that way. At the moment, she was staring at the half-eaten sandwich and half-finished cup of juice on her tray. It was like she couldn't completely function without *her* other half. I thought that was kind of weird, because it wasn't like Marilyn and Carolyn were in all the same classes together. They were apart plenty of times during the day. But somehow, just knowing that Carolyn was home while she was in school seemed to be making Marilyn feel incomplete.

"I haven't thought about that," she said. "We'd planned on doing our mirror thing together." She yawned slightly. "Sorry. I'm kind of tired. I slept in the guest room last night. Mom didn't want me catching the flu, too."

"Is the bed in the guest room uncomfortable?" Josh asked.

Marilyn shook her head. "No. It's just different."

"I know how that is," Liza said. "It's hard to get used to a new place. When I sleep at my grandmother's house, it always takes me a second to remember where I am when I wake up."

"Try moving to a new country!" Sam exclaimed. "It took me weeks to get used to waking up to a radio station where the DJs had American accents."

"Can we get back to the big problem?" Chloe urged. She turned to Marilyn. "About your spot in the variety webcast . . ."

"Maybe we should just put the webcast off for a few days, until Carolyn's better," I suggested.

"I already made up the fliers," Chloe reminded me. "And I posted them in a bunch of places. We can't change the date now."

"Oh," I said. "I forgot, sorry."

"I guess you'll have to do it without us," Marilyn said.

"Come on, Marilyn. You can come up with something," Liza urged. "Isn't there anything you've ever wanted to try?"

"Well, there is *something* I've wanted to do . . ." Marilyn began slowly. She glanced around at us.

We looked back at her, silently. None of us could finish her sentence. We had no idea what she was thinking.

"I want to make cool flip-flops," Marilyn said, finally finishing her own sentence.

"Flip-flops?" Josh asked. He sounded surprised. I guess we all were. It was such an odd thing to want to do.

Marilyn nodded. "Yeah. Now that the weather is getting warmer, there are flip-flops in all the shoe stores. Really funky decorated ones. But they're so expensive. My mom said there was no way she was buying two pairs of them."

"Crafts are fun, sure," Chloe said. "But is it good television?"

"Why not?" Sam asked. "There are all kinds of fashion and design shows on TV these days."

"They're called DIY shows," Marc said knowledgeably. "It stands for 'Do It Yourself.' "

Sam nodded. "Exactly. Marilyn could teach people how to design cool flip-flops just like the people on those shows teach people how to sew an awesome dress or make beaded earrings."

"That's a great idea!" Marilyn exclaimed. "Except . . ."

"Except what?" Liza asked her gently.

"Except I don't know how to decorate flip-flops," Marilyn said. "I'd want to make sure I was doing it right, so I don't make a fool out of myself on TV."

"Oh, that's not a problem," I assured her. "I'll call you as soon as I get home from my student council meeting."

"You know how to make cool flip-flops?" Chloe asked me.

I shook my head. "But I know where to find out how . . ."

"Middleschoolsurvival.com!" My friends all exclaimed at once.

"Now you guys are doing that twin thing." Marilyn laughed. She smiled.

"More like a septuplet thing," Josh said. "After all, there are seven of us here today."

We all started giggling. Leave it to Mr. Math to make sure we got it right.

Just as we started laughing, the Pops paraded by our table on their daily hike to the girls' room. They stopped for a minute and stared at us. At first, their peering eyes made me feel like we were laughing hyenas in a zoo. But that feeling faded quickly. The truth was, I'd rather be a laughing hyena than a painted peacock. (Which was what the Pops, with their blue eye shadow and pink lipstick, reminded me of.) Somehow I got the feeling that the hyenas had much more fun!

Chapter
FIVE

CHLOE HAD GIVEN US all a big stack of fliers to hand out that afternoon. I hadn't really gotten a chance to give out too many, so I still had plenty left when I arrived at the student council office that afternoon.

"What have you got there?" Sandee Wind, the president of the eighth grade, asked me.

"Fliers about a webcast show my friends and I are doing on Friday," I said, sliding one across the table to her.

"Oh, cool," Sandee said. "What kind of show is it going to be?"

"It's a variety show," I explained. "That's kind of like a talent show."

I glanced over to where Addie was sitting. (Addie's the vice president of the sixth grade, so she comes to all the same student council meetings I do.) She was rolling her eyes and looking incredibly bored. Like most of the Pops, Addie found any conversation that didn't focus on her boring.

"What kind of acts do you have?" Sandee asked. Obviously *she* wasn't bored.

Hah! Take that, Addie, I thought to myself. But out loud I said, "Well, my friend Chloe is going to sing, and

Josh is going to do tae kwon do and break boards with his foot —"

"I've always wanted to do that," Ethan James, the seventh grade vice president, interrupted me. Then he jumped up and did a very goofy imitation of a karate kick.

"Josh is a black belt," I told him.

"Felicia and Rachel are going to do a basketball demonstration," I continued. "Really cool stuff, like spinning the ball on their fingers, and dribbling three balls at once. And —"

"I thought we were here to talk about student council business," Addie interrupted.

"I was just getting to that," I told her. "I'm getting one minute to talk about things that are happening at school. I'm planning on reminding everyone to come to the girls' gymnastics meet next week, and I'm announcing the Spanish club's bake sale. But that still leaves me with lots of on-air time to fill. So if anybody knows about any club events, let me know and I'll announce them during the webcast."

"Awesome!" Sandee exclaimed. "It would be a big help if you could remind people to bring in new or slightly used books for the book drive we're having this month. We're going to bring the books over to the family shelter on Elm Street."

I wrote the words *book drive* on a sheet of paper in my notebook.

"And the chess club is looking for new members," John

Benson, the eighth grade vice president, told me. "Everyone from beginners to chess champs is welcome."

I wrote down *chess club* on my sheet of paper.

"And could you remind people that we're still looking for volunteers for Park Clean-Up Day?" Kia Samson, the seventh grade president, asked me. "It's a week from Sunday, and we want to get a lot of kids there to help."

"Will do," I assured her as I scribbled down *park clean-up day*.

"How about you, Addie?" Sandee asked her. "Anything you or your friends want Jenny to announce on" – she glanced down at the flier – "*Webcast Underground?*"

Addie sighed. "No, we're good," she assured Sandee.

I could have predicted that answer. The Pops weren't big on extracurricular activities. What was Addie going to suggest I announce – Don't Forget to Bring Your Green Eye Shadow Day?

But I didn't say that. Instead, I said, "Well, if you think of something before Friday, just let me know."

Addie didn't reply. But the look in her eyes let me know exactly what she was thinking. It was clear that Addie would rather die than have me announce any Pop events on *Webcast Underground.* Which was fine with me. I didn't have a great desire to help the Pops out, anyway.

Marilyn and I took the late bus home together that evening. She had stayed after school for extra help with Spanish and I'd had the student council meeting, so our timing was perfect. I could tell Marilyn was glad to have someone to ride next to on the school bus. Usually Carolyn was right there in the seat beside her.

"Weird day, huh?" I asked.

Marilyn nodded. "It just feels different without Carolyn at school," she told me. "I know that must sound strange to you but . . ." her voice trailed off.

"I feel weird when *any* of us is absent," I assured her. "It's like a piece of the puzzle is missing."

"Exactly," Marilyn said.

"Carolyn will be better soon," I told her.

"I know," Marilyn agreed. "She's going to be bummed about missing the webcast. I'm bummed, too. It would have been fun to do the mirror thing with her."

"Making fancy flip-flops will be fun, too," I told Marilyn. "And you can make a pair for Carolyn to wear when she gets back to school."

"True," Marilyn agreed. "I just hope it's not too complicated."

"Only one way to find out," I said. "As soon as we get home we'll take a look at middleschoolsurvival.com."

Which is exactly what we did. And just as I'd suspected, there were plenty of ideas for decorating your own flip-flops. Some were really difficult, but Marilyn and I were able to find one that was just right.

"Those feathery ones are adorable," Marilyn said, looking at the picture on the screen. "I hope I can do it."

"You can. It doesn't sound tough," I assured her. And it really didn't. In fact, it seemed kind of simple.

Fancy Feathery Flip-Flops

These feather-covered flip-flops are so cute, you'll want to fly to the mall to get a pair. But you'd better point your wings toward the craft store instead. These aren't available in shoe stores. You'll have to make them yourself.

YOU WILL NEED:

1 pair of plain flip-flops, fast-drying craft glue, and 1 package of colorful feathers (or an old feather boa)

HERE'S WHAT YOU DO:

1. Make sure the flip-flops are clean and dry.
2. Start at the bottom of one of the flip-flop straps. Glue your feathers in place, one by one, working your way up toward the center.
3. Repeat this process for the other strap on the same shoe. Eventually the feathers will meet in the center.
4. Fill in any gaps on the straps with more glue and feathers.
5. Now repeat steps 2–4 on the second flip-flop.
6. Allow the glue to dry for at least two hours before you wear your fine new feather flip-flops.

"I think I can do that!" Marilyn exclaimed. "In fact, I have a pair of flip-flops that I can practice on. I'll use the feathers from that black boa I wore for Halloween two years ago. And plain flip-flops aren't expensive. I can probably get my dad to take me to the mall tonight to get a couple of pairs and a big bag of feathers from the craft store."

"Great!" I exclaimed. "You'll want to practice a lot before the webcast."

"Definitely," Marilyn agreed. "I want this to be perfect!"

As we printed out the instructions, I smiled to myself. Marilyn seemed really happy. We'd found directions for creating cool flip-flops that she could make all by herself. And I think that made her feel really good.

I silently added another rule to my list of middle school rules you don't find in the handbook.

MIDDLE SCHOOL RULE #32:

WHILE IT'S GREAT TO HAVE FRIENDS (AND FAMILY) YOU CAN COUNT ON, YOU SHOULD NEVER BECOME SO DEPENDENT ON THEM THAT YOU'RE UNHAPPY WHEN THEY'RE NOT AROUND. IT'S IMPORTANT TO BE ABLE TO STAND ON YOUR OWN TWO FEET.

"Jenny, you know, I think I'd better go," Marilyn told me. "I promised my mom I would be home before dark, since I have to walk. Mom can't leave Carolyn to come pick me up."

"Okay," I told her. "Call me later and let me know how your flip-flops turn out."

"Definitely!" Marilyn assured me.

As Marilyn picked up her sweater and raced out the door I could tell she was definitely standing on her own two feet. In fact, she was so excited to get home to try out her new hobby, she was running on them!

Chapter
SIX

"CHLOE, CAN'T YOU DO ANYTHING about that dryer?" Marc shouted angrily. It was Friday night, and we were all getting snappy with one another. I guess we were nervous about the live webcast we were about to do.

"My mom says she has to finish the load that's in there," Chloe said. "It's not so loud."

"The microphone on the computer is picking it up," Marc insisted.

"So move the computer," Chloe suggested.

"He can't," Liza told Chloe. "I've got the whole set arranged. If he moves the computer, I'll have to redo everything. And I'm definitely not doing that."

"Why don't we just wait until the dryer stops to do the webcast?" I suggested.

"Because we said eight o'clock on all the fliers," Chloe told me. She sounded annoyed that I'd even brought it up.

"You mean *you* said eight o'clock," I reminded her. "You made up the fliers without even asking what time we wanted —" I stopped myself mid-sentence, realizing I sounded angry, too. And I wasn't angry. I was just really,

really, nervous. I shut my mouth and looked back down at my news report notecards.

"Ow!" I heard Josh shout from the other end of the basement.

"What happened?" Felicia asked, racing over to him.

"I hit my practice board with the wrong part of my foot," he explained.

"Are you hurt?" Felicia asked.

"You'd better not be," Chloe said. "Your wood-breaking thing is a major part of my show."

"*Your* show?" Marc asked her. "I'm the director."

"I meant *our* show," Chloe assured him. "Boy, Marc. You're so touchy today."

"Oops!" Just then we all heard Marilyn shout from the corner of the room. I looked over. She was surrounded by a mountain of feathers. "I spilled all the feathers in the bag," she said nervously.

Liza ran over to help her gather them up again.

"You have to be careful," Felicia told her. "We don't need feathers flying all around the set during the webcast."

"Sorry," Marilyn said. She sounded really stressed-out. "I'm getting them all up now. There won't be any left on the floor of the laundry room, I promise."

Marc growled and rested his forehead in his hand. "It's not a laundry room, it's a studio!" he shouted at Marilyn.

"It's both," Liza reminded him.

"Ruff! Ruff!" Just then, Bingo came bounding down the stairs to see what all the noise was about.

"Chloe!" Marc shouted. "Do something about that mutt!"

"He's not a mutt. He's a mixed breed," Chloe insisted. "And he'll quiet down in a minute, if you'll just stop yelling!"

Suddenly, I wasn't nervous anymore. I just wanted it to be eight o'clock already so we could start the webcast. No matter how bad our show turned out to be, it would never be worse than all this fighting!

"Okay, places everyone," Marc said, looking at his watch. "Thirty seconds until airtime!"

I could feel the butterflies in my stomach begin to flutter.

"Action," Marc said, pointing to Chloe. "Welcome to *Webcast Underground*," she said into the camera. "We're here to entertain all of you! I'm going to start the show off with a song. I think you'll all know it."

Liza reached over and clicked on Chloe's MP3 player. As the music played, Chloe began to sing "Dancing Queen." "You can dance, you can jive, having the time of your life . . ."

As Chloe sang, I turned my attention to Marilyn. She was on next. At least she was supposed to be. But I couldn't tell if she'd be able to do it. Her eyes were wide open with fear. Her skin had faded to a chalky white.

"Are you okay?" I whispered to her, keeping my voice really low so the microphone wouldn't pick up the sound. Not that I really had to worry about that.

I was standing next to the dryer, and it was louder than I was.

"I'm nervous," Marilyn whispered back. "I've never done anything like this."

"None of us have," I assured her.

"Will you do it with me?" Marilyn asked.

I shook my head. "I'd probably just mess it all up."

"But I'm not good at doing things on my own," Marilyn insisted. "And with all the people who are watching us, it's even scarier."

I knew what she meant. I was feeling the same way. But I knew I couldn't tell Marilyn that. I had to act like I wasn't scared so she wouldn't be scared, either. After all, she was the next act. And if she didn't go on, there would be nothing on the screen. That would be really embarrassing for all of us.

"You won't be alone," I assured her. "I'll go stand right behind the computer. If you get freaked out, just look at me."

Marilyn took a deep breath. "I guess that would help," she said.

"Then you'll do the same thing for me, okay?" I asked her.

"Deal," Marilyn agreed.

As Chloe's song came to an end, I quickly raced behind the computer and stood beside Marc. At the same time, Liza hurried over and helped Marilyn move her craft materials to a table that was already set up near where Chloe had been singing.

Marilyn looked up at me. I flashed her a huge smile. She gave me a nervous smile in return. Then she looked down at the table, picked up a flip-flop and some feathers, and got ready to begin her demonstration.

"Ruff! Ruff!" Just then, Bingo came racing over. He began to bark at Marilyn's feet. I could see Marilyn starting to panic again. So could Chloe. So she rushed over and grabbed Bingo. Then she jumped in front of Marilyn and smiled at the computer.

"This is Bingo," Chloe said, making her dog wave his paw up and down. "He's really excited because Marilyn is about to show everyone how to make the coolest flip-flops ever!"

As soon as she finished talking, Chloe took Bingo upstairs and shut the door tight. I could hear him scratching at the door, but I didn't think the audience would be able to. Wow! Chloe sure had been able to think fast. Making Bingo seem like part of the cast had been absolute genius. She'd acted like a real pro.

Marilyn wasn't doing too badly, either. As soon as she began arranging the feathers on the straps of the flip-flops, she started to relax. In fact, she seemed to be having a lot of fun. "Start at the bottom of the strap," she said with a grin as she glued a bright yellow feather onto her orange flip-flop. "And then add the next one."

About a minute or two later, Marilyn was already work-ing on the second flip-flop. Her act was going off without a hitch.

Gulp. I knew what that meant. The flip-flops were almost finished. And once they were, it would be my turn to go on.

Sure enough, less than a minute later, I found myself sitting behind the table, giving my news broadcast. I tried not to look at my note cards, and made a real effort to smile every now and then, the way the real newscasters on TV do.

"It's book drive time," I said. "Please bring your new and gently used books for kids of all ages to the Joyce Kilmer Middle School Book Drive. They will be donated to our local family shelter." I took a breath, and then switched note cards. "On a sports note, the Joyce Kilmer Middle School girls' gymnastics team will —"

Buzzzz. Before I could finish my sentence, a buzzer went off in our studio. My eyes opened wide. I had no idea what that was.

"It just means the dryer's done," Chloe mouthed silently. "Keep going."

The dryer buzzer threw me for a second, but I found my bearings pretty quickly, and I was able to finish my news minute without any other problems. It hadn't been too difficult, but I was definitely glad when it was over. Chloe may have loved being on camera and performing, but the whole thing made me nervous. I was happy that after my part in the show, I was able to sit back and watch Felicia and Rachel spin their basketballs on their fingers and dribble between their legs. I like being in the audience a lot more than being onstage. That's cool, though. You need both performers and audience members to make a show, right?

Speaking of audiences, we obviously had a big one on Friday night, because as I got off the school bus on Monday morning, I was greeted by lots of fans. It seemed like everyone had seen our *Webcast Underground* show.

"Great show, you guys," Kia congratulated us. "Thanks for mentioning all the student council stuff, Jenny."

I grinned. "Just doing my job," I told her.

"Are you going to do another show?" John asked. "Because I have a whole list of things you can announce."

"I don't know," I told him honestly. "We really only planned the first one."

"You should definitely do more," Kia said. She held up her foot. "I even tried to make feather flip-flops like Marilyn did. Mine came out okay. Not as good as hers, but I'm not an expert like she is."

I struggled not to laugh. Marilyn wasn't an expert, either. She'd only just learned to do it. But I was glad she had been able to fool our audience.

Just then, Chloe, Marc, and Josh walked over to where I was standing. They were surrounded by lots of kids.

"How long have you been taking tae kwon do?" I heard one guy with short blond curls ask Josh.

"Since I was in kindergarten," Josh told him. "But there are lots of older kids who are just beginning at my tae kwon do school."

"Will I get to break boards the first day?" the blond kid wondered. "I was blown away when you jumped up and just smashed through those two thick boards."

"Thanks," Josh said, blushing slightly. "You won't be able to break thick boards right away, but eventually you will. They start you off with thinner boards until you get the hang of it."

"Your tae kwon do act was definitely one of the best moments of your show," a girl named Jada, who I recognized from my gym class, told Josh. Then she looked at the rest of us. "You were all good, of course."

"By the way, Chloe, have you seen my sweatshirt?" Felicia asked, obviously wanting to change the subject from Jada's fawning over Josh. "I must have left it in your basement."

Chloe shook her head. "I didn't notice it, but I'll look for it tonight." She turned her attention back to Jada. "Did you like anything else besides the tae kwon do?" she asked pointedly.

Jada looked uncomfortable. "Um, sure. Your singing was great. And so was your basketball routine, Felicia."

"Thanks," Chloe replied, perking up the minute Jada mentioned her singing.

At that moment, the first warning bell rang. It was time for us to go inside. After all, even Internet stars like us have to get to class on time.

I made it to English class with only a minute to spare. But that was just long enough to overhear Addie and Dana talking about our webcast. I was surprised that they'd even watched it. But I *wasn't* surprised at their reaction to it.

"Chloe hit some clunkers in that song," Dana said, without even bothering to lower her voice.

I glanced over at Chloe. She looked calm and happy. If she'd heard Dana's comment, she wasn't reacting to it.

"And how about Felicia and Rachel?" Addie asked Dana. "Who wants to watch them bounce a ball?"

I wanted to tell Addie that it's really hard to dribble a basketball back and forth between your legs, and that Felicia and Rachel had been practicing all week to get their routine timed perfectly, but I didn't. There was no way I was going to let Addie and Dana think their conversation was getting to me. I was going to ignore them. That's the way Chloe handles the Pops, and I've always admired her for it.

"How about when the buzzer from the dryer went off in the middle of the newscast?" Dana giggled. "I'm cracking up just remembering it."

I frowned. There was no arguing with Dana there. The buzzer going off *had* been pretty bad.

"Frankly, I think the dog was the best part," Dana

continued. "At least he barked in one key. That's more than I could say for Chloe. Talent show? More like an *un*-talent show if you ask me."

Now I was getting mad. I opened my mouth to say something, but Chloe touched my arm. "They're just jealous," she whispered to me. "Ignore them."

I don't know how Chloe does it. She really didn't seem at all bothered by Addie and Dana. Besides, she was right. They probably were jealous of all the attention our webcast was getting. The Pops weren't used to anyone else being the center of attention.

"I don't know why people are so excited about that show," Addie said. "But soon the whole *Webcast Underground* mess will be over. Everyone will forget about it, once we unveil *our* surprise!"

At just that moment, Ms. Jaffe, our English teacher, walked into the classroom. That meant Addie and Dana had to be quiet. So I wasn't going to get to hear anything more about their surprise. Which meant I only knew two things for sure: One, the Pops were up to something. And two, whatever it was, it wasn't going to make my friends and me very happy. Nothing the Pops came up with ever did.

Chapter
SEVEN

I DIDN'T HAVE TO WAIT long to find out what the Pops' surprise was. When I got to lunch, Marc, Josh, Liza, Marilyn, and Carolyn were looking at a pink flier.

"Did you see this?" Marilyn asked me.

"I had one handed to me on the way out of gym," Carolyn added. She didn't sound stuffed up at all.

"I'm glad you're feeling better," I told her.

"Me, too," Carolyn said. "But wait until you read this. Then *you* might feel a little sick."

I took the pink piece of paper from her and read it.

WHAT ARE THE COOLEST KIDS IN SCHOOL WEARING?

There's only one way to find out.
Watch SCHOOL STYLE!
Thursday night at 7:00 P.M.!

"Let me guess," Sam said. "It's a Pop webcast."

I nodded. "That would be my guess. After all, they're the coolest kids in school."

"At least *they* think they are," Sam corrected me.

Chloe snatched the paper from me. "This is stupid," she proclaimed. "Who wants to watch the Pops show off their clothes? We see them in school every day."

Chloe just didn't get it. Everybody wanted to look like the Pops. Everyone except Chloe, that is. She was happy wearing jeans and T-shirts. Her shirt today was especially funny. It said *I'm a legend in my own mind.*

"They're such copycats," Liza said.

"Seriously. They wouldn't know an original idea if it bit them on the nose," Sam agreed.

I sighed. It didn't matter if the Pops had started this whole webcast thing or not. The truth was, after Thursday night, all anyone would remember was *School Style. Webcast Underground* would be totally forgotten.

Apparently, Chloe had the same fear. But she wasn't going down without a fight. "Their show is Thursday, right?" she asked. We nodded. "Fine. But our next show is Friday. And we're going to do something spectacular."

"I didn't know we were doing a next show," Marc said.

"Oh, we are," Chloe said. "And we're going to get a much bigger audience than the Pops will."

"How are we going to do that?" Josh asked her.

"I haven't figured that part out yet," Chloe admitted.

"But I'm sure we can come up with something. We're much smarter than the Pops."

"That's true," Josh agreed. He pointed to Marc. "And we have Mr. Spielberg over here to make sure of it."

Marc laughed. "Well, I don't know about being like Steven Spielberg. But I do know a thing or two about making a good show. And the first thing I can tell you is you have to get the audience involved. You have to make them want to come back and watch again and again."

"Exactly!" Chloe exclaimed. "And I know we can do it!"

I sighed as I listened to my friends planning the next episode of *Webcast Underground.* They were all so certain that they could come up with something that would top the Pops' show. I only hoped they were right.

That evening, I couldn't focus on my homework. I kept thinking about what Marc had said. We needed to make the audience want to come back again. But how? We'd all done our best on the first show. I wasn't sure what we could do that wouldn't make our second show seem like a rerun of the first.

I was feeling frustrated, so I was glad when Rachel called. "Hey, Rach," I greeted her.

"Hi, Jenny," she replied. "Did Chloe tell you we're doing another episode of *Webcast Underground* on Friday?"

"Yeah," I answered. "She's pretty much told everyone."

"Are you doing the newscast again?" Rachel asked me.

"I guess so. What are you and Felicia planning?"

Rachel was quiet for a minute. "Felicia's actually helping Josh with a new tae kwon do demonstration. She's holding boards for him to break, and then announcing what he's going to try next," she said finally. "So that kind of leaves me on my own."

"Oh," I replied. I wasn't quite sure what to say next. I could tell by the tone of her voice that Rachel was bummed that Felicia had decided to do an act with her boyfriend instead of with her.

"I might do a comedy act instead," Rachel continued.

"That's a great idea!" I exclaimed, trying to sound really supportive.

"Yeah, well, I figured you guys all think I'm funny, so why wouldn't everybody else?" Rachel pointed out. "But I can't decide what kind of comedy act to do."

"What do you mean?" I asked her.

"There are lots of kinds of comedy," Rachel explained. "There's slapstick, like when people get hit with a pie or slip on a banana peel. And there's stand-up, which is when someone gets up and tells jokes. And then there's irony humor. That's the toughest one because you don't really tell jokes. You just sort of point out all the weird, bizarre things in everyday life."

"Wow!" I exclaimed. And I meant it. I'd really had no idea that there were different kinds of comedy.

"Being a comedian is serious business, Jenny," Rachel told me.

"I guess so," I replied. "What kind of act are you going to do?"

"That's what I've been trying to figure out," Rachel said. "I don't know which I'd be best at. I wish someone could just tell me what kind of comedian to be."

"Maybe middleschoolsurvival.com has a quiz to help you figure it out," I suggested.

"I doubt it," Rachel said. "I mean how many middle school comedians are there?"

I didn't know the answer to that one, but I did know that my favorite website had never let me down before. So I went straight to the site and started searching the quizzes. Sure enough, in a matter of seconds, I'd found exactly what I was looking for!

"Here's a great quiz," I told Rachel. "It's just what you're looking for."

"Awesome!" Rachel exclaimed. "Let's get started."

What Tickles Your Funny Bone?

Have you ever wondered why your best friend laughs at a cartoon character slipping on a banana peel, while you laugh at knock-knock jokes? Take this quiz and you'll figure out what your comedy style is.

1. When you and your pals get together, what's your favorite game to play?

A. Balderdash. There's something funny about watching people have so much trouble bluffing — even though it's a game where you're supposed to bluff!

B. Truth or dare. The last time you played you dared someone to walk around outside with her clothes on backward. It was hilarious!

C. Charades. Acting things out and imitating famous people is your idea of a laugh.

"Hmm . . ." Rachel murmured as she began to figure out her options, "I'm terrible at Balderdash. I always pick the made-up definition for the word instead of the real one. And I tried playing charades with my cousin a few months ago, and I couldn't get anyone to guess the movie I was supposed to act out. It was *Peter Pan*, and nobody could figure out I was trying to fry stuff in a pan."

I actually thought *Peter Pan* was a really hard charade to act out, so that probably hadn't been Rachel's fault. But I didn't want to influence her, so I didn't say anything.

"I guess I'd have to say B," Rachel decided finally. "It would actually be pretty funny to see someone walking around with their clothes on backward."

"B it is," I said, clicking my computer mouse. A moment later, the next question popped up on the screen.

2. Your gym teacher was demonstrating how to do a layup in basketball and she fell right on her butt. What's your reaction?

A. Snicker quietly in the back of the crowd. There's something hilarious about a gym teacher who can't play sports.

B. Laugh hysterically. What could be funnier than seeing a teacher making a totally klutzy move like that?

C. You don't dare giggle in front of the teacher. But you act out the whole thing for your friends later on.

"Definitely C," Rachel said. "I have Coach O for gym, and he can get pretty mean. If I laughed at him and got caught, it'd be detention for sure. But I would have to act it out for you guys later. I mean, I couldn't keep something that funny to myself, could I?"

"I hope not," I said as I clicked the letter C on the computer screen. "I'd really want to hear all about that."

3. **At the talent show, you and your friends put on a funny skit. What kind of skit is it?**

A. A strange dance number in which you do hip-hop moves and run around the stage dressed as kangaroos and bunnies while classical ballet music plays in the background.

B. A fake knife-throwing act in which you keep missing and fake blood spurts out from your friend, the victim.

C. A make-believe red carpet interview in which you and your pals make fun of all the teachers.

"C again," Rachel said. "Can't you just see us doing that? Chloe does an incredible Ms. Jaffe imitation. And I can definitely picture myself pretending to be Mr. Collins. He's the funniest school janitor in the world."

I remembered how nice Mr. Collins had been to me on the first day of school. He'd helped me find the cafeteria after a group of eighth graders had sent me on a wild-goose chase looking for an elevator that didn't exist. I didn't know if Mr. Collins was funny, but he was helpful.

"Okay, here's the next one," I told Rachel as a new quiz question appeared on my screen.

4. Your best friend just got a pet parrot. What is it about him that cracks you up the most?

A. His name. She called her bird Fido!

B. The fact that he's a flying disaster. He's already broken a lamp and pooped on her brother's head!

C. His voice. He sounds remarkably like that weird guy who sits three rows behind you in math class.

Rachel began to giggle. "All those answers are hysterical," she told me. "I don't know which to choose." She laughed even harder — so hard that she actually snorted! That started me laughing, too. It took us a long time to get all the giggles out of our systems.

"Okay, um . . . which one was the thing about his weird voice?" Rachel asked, as she choked back another round of giggles. "Because I do know a kid who sounds like a parrot. It's hilarious."

"C," I said, wiping a few laugh-related tears out of my eyes, too.

"Then, C," she said.

"Okay," I said, clicking the C.

5. During a trip to the zoo, which animals do you enjoy watching the most?

A. The tigers. They think they're so fierce, but the humans have them trapped in cages.

B. The monkeys. They make such goofy faces at the people.

C. The people. Watching them make faces and say funny things to the animals can be extremely entertaining.

"Oh, B, totally!" Rachel exclaimed. "The monkeys are my favorite zoo animals. They crack me up."

I clicked my mouse over the letter B. A moment later a new image appeared on my screen.

You chose 0 A'S, 2 B'S, and 3 C'S.
So what do your answers say about your sense of humor?

Mostly A's: Satire's your idea of humor. You find humor in the little ironies of life. Lucky you, because that kind of humor is all around you all the time.

Mostly B's: You have a slapstick sensibility. There's nothing like a pie smashing in someone's face to get you giggling.

Mostly C's: You're a stand-up kinda gal — stand-up comedy, that is. You have a great appreciation for a well-told joke.

Rachel thought about that for a minute. "Stand-up comedy, huh?" she said out loud. "Well, I am a good joke teller."

I was glad Rachel and I were on the phone instead of in the same room. I think she might have been insulted by the way I'd wrinkled my nose at her statement. Sometimes Rachel can tell a funny joke. But often her jokes are pretty bad. My friends and I are pretty nice about laughing at her jokes (at least most of the time), but I wasn't sure the Pops or other kids in the webcast viewing audience would be as kind.

"I could work up a routine of jokes and tell them," Rachel continued.

"Well, you could . . ." I began slowly, not sure how to broach this subject with Rachel.

"But on the other hand, I did give two B answers. And that means I would be good at doing slapstick stuff, too," she continued.

"I guess," I said.

"But slapstick's pretty hard to do on your own." Rachel continued to think out loud. "Ooh! I have a great idea. Maybe you can help me with it."

I wasn't sure I liked the sound of that, but I figured it couldn't hurt to hear Rachel's idea.

"What if I started out telling jokes, and then you could come by and smash a pie in my face?" Rachel asked me. "It would be really funny because it would be a total surprise, and because it would seem like you didn't think my jokes were funny. That would actually be irony, because of course my jokes would be hilarious."

I didn't know about *that*, but I could see where a pie in the face could be really funny – and really messy.

"Are you sure you won't mind getting a face full of whipped cream?" I asked her.

"Totally," Rachel assured me. "I love whipped cream. And maybe we can mix some chocolate pudding in there, too. Make it really gross. We may as well go all the way."

"No sacrifice is too great for *Webcast Underground*," I teased.

"Exactly," Rachel agreed. "Besides, I love chocolate pudding! Which reminds me. Do you know why the sergeant refused to pass chocolate pudding to the soldier?"

"Why?" I asked her.

"Because it's against regulations to help another soldier to dessert!" Rachel exclaimed. Then she burst out laughing at her own joke.

I rolled my eyes. Oh, boy. With jokes like that we'd need a lot more than a pie to make our show more successful than the Pops' show. We'd need a whole bakery!

Chapter

EIGHT

OKAY, I ADMIT IT. Even though the Pops are basically the sworn enemies of my group of friends, I watched *School Style* on Thursday night. I couldn't help myself. I was curious to see what it would be like. And I suspect almost everyone else in the school felt the same way. That was how the Pops affected the non-Pops. We all wanted a little glimpse into what life as a Pop was like. And that was why at seven o'clock I was glued to my computer instead of reading my history book.

School Style started out with a song we'd all been hearing on the radio lately. It was kind of bouncy and really danceable, which explained why all of the Pops were bopping around in front of the camera while it played. The Pops didn't have a talented artist like Liza to make a cool set for them, or a directing whiz like Marc to adjust the lighting and sound, so Maya, Claire, Dana, Sabrina, and Addie looked like they were dancing around someone's unfinished basement.

Still, I couldn't help watching – at least for a little while. But before long, I got really bored. There was nothing new about it. The Pops on a webcast were pretty much like the Pops in real life. They were obsessed with makeup, clothes, and themselves. And they spent the whole web-cast just sitting around talking about those things. There wasn't any singing, or feathered flip-flops, or even bas-ketball tricks. There was just a whole lot of talk.

The Pops' broadcast gabfest didn't reveal any big sur-prises – unless you were the kind of person who was amazed to discover that Sabrina thought purple eyeliner brought out brown eyes, or that Addie sometimes liked to sprinkle glitter in her hair for some "extra sparkle." And then of course there was the big breaking news alert from Dana – next year low-rise jeans would totally be out, and people would be wearing jeans with high waistlines.

Personally, I didn't find any of those things interest-ing. However, I was apparently in the minority because the next morning I saw a lot of girls wearing higher-waisted jeans, purple eyeliner, and glitter in their hair. Such is the power of the Pops.

Chloe wasn't one of the kids who'd been taken in by *School Style*, though. When I came into English class on Friday morning, she was wearing a pair of faded overalls and sneakers. There was no glitter in her hair at all.

Sam hadn't been influenced by the Pop fashion reports, either. She wasn't wearing high-waisted jeans or eye shadow. Instead, she was dressed in pink-and-black zebra-patterned leggings and a long black sweater. She also had a streak of pink dye in her hair, which was way cooler than any glitter Addie might wear. Sam was the only per-son in our school cool enough to pull off a look like that.

It was really impressive. And I wasn't the only one who thought so. The Pops did, too. I could tell because they never gave her any grief about her clothes.

"Oh, man, that show was a total train wreck!" Chloe exclaimed as she sat down at the desk next to me. I glanced at the seats near the windows, where Addie and Dana usually sat. I was sort of hoping they'd heard what Chloe had said. But Addie and Dana weren't in class yet. I figured they were still in the hall being greeted by their adoring (glittery!) public.

"We're totally going to outdo them tonight," Chloe continued. "Wait until I tell you what Marc and I worked out for our big surprise. It's going to be incredible!"

Sam and I moved closer, eager to hear Chloe's plan. But before she could say a word, Addie and Dana slithered into the room. They shot Chloe, Sam, and I big smiles as they walked past. Obviously they were very pleased with the reaction their webcast had gotten.

"I'd better tell you guys the plan when we meet at my house after school," Chloe said. "I wouldn't want our surprise to get into enemy hands. That could be devastating to our side."

Enemy hands. Our side. The words rang in my head. *Webcast Underground* had started out as a fun thing to do on a Friday evening. Now, somehow, it had turned into a war between my friends and the Pops. *Just like everything else in middle school.*

*   *   *

"We're having a *singing* contest?" my voice scaled up nervously as I repeated what Chloe had just said during our preshow meeting in her laundry room that evening.

"Exactly," Chloe said. "It's the perfect idea. We get audience participation, which makes people want to tune in."

"But I can't sing," I told her.

"Neither can I," Rachel pointed out.

"You're the only one of us who sings, Chloe," Felicia said. "Except maybe Sam. She has a really good voice. I heard her singing along with her MP3 player one day. I didn't know she was so musical."

"I didn't know, either," Rachel said. "But it doesn't surprise me. Well, actually it kind of does. Everything about Sam surprises me."

"Sam's not here," Chloe said, bristling at the idea that someone else in our group could sing. "She's not allowed to come, because she's still arguing with her mom."

"What's that about, anyway?" Liza asked.

"She said it had something to do with . . ." Marilyn began.

". . . some lessons her mom wanted her to take," Carolyn finished the thought.

"But she didn't say what kind of lessons," they explained together.

I smiled. It was good to have the twins back together and sounding normal. Well, normal for the twins, anyhow.

"Sam's problems don't matter right now," Chloe reminded us. "What matters is this contest. And you guys don't have to sing, so you can just relax. The contest is only for audience members. No one who is part of the show can actually win."

"How is this going to work?" Liza asked.

"Simple," Chloe said.

That made me nervous, because Chloe's plans are never simple. They're usually complicated, which makes them a disaster in the long run.

"We ask people to e-mail videos of themselves singing to us," Chloe explained. "Then we pick five finalists. The finalists get to perform live on our webcast. And then the audience members will vote online."

"The winner gets to make a music video, which I'll direct," Marc explained.

I had to admit, that *did* seem pretty simple.

"There is one problem," Josh pointed out.

Uh-oh.

"When the people come to perform on the show, who's going to accompany them?" Josh asked. "We can't fit a band down here."

Chloe smiled. "Marc and I already thought of that," she told Josh. She pulled her MP3 player out of her pocket. "I'm going to record all kinds of karaoke background tracks on here. The finalists will sing along with those tracks. They can pick their song from the list on my computer."

Josh nodded. Obviously, that answer satisfied him, which was a relief to me. If someone as smart as Josh was satisfied, so was I.

"Okay, if no one has any other questions, we should probably start getting ready for the show," Marc said. "We only have half an hour until showtime."

That half hour went quickly because there was so much for us to do. Liza had to put the curtain back up to cover the stairs, Marc had to adjust the lighting in the room, the twins had to go over their mirror act, Felicia had to hold practice boards for Josh, and Chloe had to warm up her voice.

"Ma mi mi ma moo," Chloe sang out as she exercised her vocal cords. "Ma mi mi ma moo . . ." That part of her warm up was actually pretty funny, but none of us laughed. We all knew how seriously Chloe took her singing. In fact, the idea of her letting someone who might even have a better voice than she did on our webcast was pretty impressive. It showed how badly she wanted *Webcast Underground* to be a success. She was being a real team player. You just can't laugh at a person like that.

Anyway, with everything that was going on, time totally flew by. The next thing I knew, Marc was shouting out, "Places everyone. Thirty seconds until showtime."

Our second webcast was definitely more organized than the first one. For one thing, Chloe had convinced her mom to let the laundry wait until after we were finished broadcasting. Bingo had been relegated to the den upstairs. And much to my surprise, our acts were even better than they had been on the first show. Chloe sang a medley of songs from cartoon movies, and she didn't hit one wrong note. Josh did an amazing flying leap, and he was able to break two boards at the same time — one with each foot. The twins' mirror act was a definite highlight. They didn't miss a beat as they mimicked each other's movements. I couldn't tell one girl from the other, and I was sitting right there in the room with them. I could only imagine how amazing it must have looked to the kids sitting at home watching on their computers.

Finally, it was time for Rachel's act. She got up in front of the camera and smiled. "Good evening, ladies and germs," she joked. "It's so great to be back on *Webcast Underground*. Of course, shooting a show underground has its own problems. For instance, there are worms. They *live* underground, you know. But I must say that hanging out with worms has taught me a lot about them. For instance, did you hear about the glowworm that was unhappy? Her children weren't all that bright!"

She waited for a second, obviously leaving time for her audience to laugh. So we laughed, even though none of us thought the joke was very funny.

"I've also learned about a new breed of worms that scientists created when they crossed an earthworm with an elephant," Rachel continued. "Boy does it leave huge holes in your garden!"

Ouch! That joke was so bad, even *we* were having trouble laughing.

"And did you hear what the woodworm said to the chair?" Rachel asked. "It's been nice gnawing you!"

That was it. I had to put a stop to the bad jokes right now! Quickly, I raced onto the set and smashed our chocolate whipped cream mush pie right into Rachel's face.

At first no one in the basement said anything. Rachel and I hadn't warned them about what we were going to do, so they were just as surprised as the kids at home. A moment later, they started giggling – especially when Rachel used her finger to scoop some pudding off of her nose and pop it into her mouth. "Mmmm . . . chocolatey," she cooed. That really cracked everyone up.

Rachel grinned into the camera. She was obviously pleased that her slapstick surprise had been a success. "And speaking of chocolate . . ." she began.

But I stopped her. "Oh, no, you don't," I said in a teasing tone. "Your act is over. Now it's time for the news. Chloe, I think you have a big announcement for everyone."

As Chloe walked in front of the computer camera, she made a point of not looking at Rachel. Not that I blamed her. I knew that one look at Rachel's chocolate and whipped cream covered face would send her right back to giggling. And Chloe didn't want to giggle now. Her announcement was too important!

"Thanks, Jenny," Chloe said. "I do have a huge

announcement for all the kids at Joyce Kilmer Middle School. Especially you kids who've always dreamed about making your own music video! We've got a contest for you! All you have to do is e-mail us a video of yourself singing. The cast of *Webcast Underground* will choose five finalists. The finalists will all appear on next week's *Webcast Underground.* And then it's up to our audience to choose just who will be *Webcast Underground*'s Top Singing Star. That lucky person will win a spectacular prize – the chance to shoot a music video directed by *Webcast Underground*'s very own Marc Newman!"

My friends and I all applauded, which made Marc blush. But he turned even redder when Chloe added, "Come on out here, Marc!"

Marc shook his head, hard. Like Liza, he preferred to be behind the scenes whenever possible.

But Chloe wasn't giving up. "Come on, Marc, show your face. You're going to be a big part of making our winner a star!"

A star? Once again, Chloe was exaggerating. Getting a chance to sing on a middle school webcast and make a video directed by a member of the school film club wasn't exactly stardom. At least not the way people usually thought of it. Still, I had to admire Chloe's enthusiasm. And she wasn't entirely wrong. At the moment, Joyce Kilmer Middle School was our world. So if someone could be famous with the kids at school, it was sort of like being a star to us, anyway.

Marc must have realized that Chloe wasn't about to give up, because he finally stood up and walked in front of the webcam for a minute. "I'm looking forward to working with the winner," he said. Then he hurried back to his place behind the scenes.

"And I'm sure they look forward to working with you, too, Marc," Chloe told him. Then she pointed her finger toward our invisible audience. "And we all look forward to seeing your videos! So start e-mailing them to us right away. We'll contact you to let you know if you're a finalist."

A few seconds later, Marc shouted, "And we're out." The webcast was over.

"Well, that went well," Chloe said. "I'll bet we're going to get tons of responses to the contest."

Chloe seemed really excited. But suddenly an uncomfortable feeling washed over me. What if we didn't get a lot of videos? What if we didn't get any? How embarrassing would it be if we threw a contest and nobody entered it?

I guess I didn't really have to worry about that, because by Saturday afternoon my e-mail in-box was flooded with videos. Chloe had sent a bunch of them over to me and an equal number to my other friends.

"Can you believe how many entries we got?" Chloe exclaimed to me after I'd called her to let her know I'd gotten the e-mails. "It's like half the school wants to be a singer."

"How are we going to pick just five finalists out of all of these?" I asked her.

"Well, a lot of them aren't very good," Chloe said. "You can cross those people off right away. Then just pick your favorites of the ones that are left. If everybody does that, we'll have narrowed it down enough so that between us all we'll be able to get it down to five."

That sounded reasonable enough to me. "When do you want to meet to pick the final five?" I asked her.

"I was hoping Monday after school, if everyone's free," Chloe said. "That will give us enough time to pick the finalists and let them know."

"I'm free on Monday," I assured her.

"So is Marc," Chloe told me. "And I'll check with everyone else to make sure." She paused for a minute. "It's kind of amazing, isn't it?"

"What is?" I asked her.

"How many people are watching us," Chloe explained. "It's hard to imagine that when it's just us sitting there in my basement in front of a webcam."

"I know what you mean," I replied.

"But they're definitely watching," Chloe said. "And I think our show is more popular than that Pops show. I mean people might have tuned in the first time, just out of curiosity. But I think now that they've seen how boring the Pops can be, they'll stop watching. Nothing the Pops can do will ever be as exciting as this contest!"

I gulped. Chloe shouldn't have said that. It was almost like she was daring the Pops to do something bigger and better than we had. And even though she hadn't said it directly to them, she had thrown the idea out into the universe. I had an uneasy feeling in my stomach. Now that Chloe had actually said it out loud, I had a feeling the Pops would find a way to top what we had done.

Chapter
NINE

AND OF COURSE, I WAS RIGHT. The Pops *had* come up with something that would make sure people would come back for a second helping of *School Style*. And they hadn't waited for their next show to announce it, either. Their announcement came Saturday evening, in the form of an e-mail sent to every single person in the school.

From: Addie Wilson
Sent: Saturday, 9:04 PM
To: Joyce Kilmer Middle School
Subject: Do You Need a Major Makeover?

Let the *School Style* stars take over! Just e-mail us your picture and tell us why you should be made over. We'll choose the person we think needs the most help and we'll make them over live on our webcast. The winner will even get a chance to eat lunch with the cast of *School Style*!

My cell phone started ringing the minute the e-mail arrived. It was Felicia.

"This is getting ridiculous!" she said when I answered the phone.

I didn't have to ask what "this" was. I knew she was talking about the Pops' e-mail.

"Can't they come up with anything on their own?" Felicia demanded. "First they copy us by having a webcast. Now they're having a contest on their webcast! What is their problem?"

"*We* are," I told her. "They can't stand it when we get any attention."

"And we're definitely getting attention," Felicia said. "I have at least twenty videos to go through. So far I only like two or three of them."

"I haven't started yet," I admitted. "I kind of feel weird about judging other people's videos when I don't know anything about singing."

"You know what you like, don't you?" Felicia asked me. "Just choose the singers who sound the best."

"I guess," I agreed. "But it's just so uncomfortable. I feel like everyone who sent in a video should get some sort of prize — just for having the guts to do it."

"You are too nice, Jenny, you know that?" Felicia said. "But it's okay. It's one of the things we all like best about you. This school's got enough mean people. And most of them are in the cast of *School Style*."

I giggled. There was definitely no arguing there.

When I got to the bus stop on Monday morning, Addie was already there. She was wearing a pale blue sweater over a matching blue-and-white striped tank top and a pale blue miniskirt. I could tell she was trying to look especially stylish today – probably so she would seem more authentic as one of the makeover artists on *School Style*. Whatever the reason, it was definitely working. Addie looked like she'd popped out of the pages of a magazine.

As I walked up to the stop, Addie looked me up and down. Then she rolled her eyes. "Jenny, what are you wearing?"

I looked down at my outfit. When I'd gotten dressed this morning, I thought my dark blue jeans and red polo shirt were perfectly fine. But standing there next to Addie, I suddenly felt as dingy as a dishrag (to quote something my grandmother likes to say).

"You really should enter the *School Style* makeover contest," Addie said. "You're dressed just badly enough to get chosen. Just think – maybe if you wore the right clothes, your friends would let you spend more time on camera during your webcast."

"What's that supposed to mean?" I demanded.

Addie sighed. "Come on, Jenny. It's obvious your friends don't think you look good enough to be on TV, or they'd give you something to do. On Friday all you did was smash a pie in Rachel's face and introduce Chloe. It's obvious your friends are ashamed of you."

"They are not!" I shouted back at her. "My friends don't care about what people wear...."

"Obviously," Addie replied with a nasty giggle.

"They don't," I insisted. "We like each other for who we are, not what we wear. We're not shallow."

Addie shrugged. "Suit yourself. I'm sure there's plenty to do behind the scenes, too."

Just then the bus pulled up. I was so relieved. I was tired of arguing with Addie. Not that I thought what she was saying was true. My friends weren't ashamed of me. It was just that with the announcement of the contest, there hadn't been time for my newscast. That was why I hadn't been on camera much.

I knew that for sure. I really did. But for some reason, Addie's words stuck with me all day. They followed me all the way to Chloe's house that afternoon, where my friends and I settled in to pick the five finalists for our contest.

"This is a really tough job," Sam said as we watched a video of an eighth grader named Alicia singing an old Beatles tune. "I mean, this girl stays on key pretty well, but her rhythm is off. And sometimes her pitch is wrong. But she's pretty good. They all are. I don't know how we're going to choose just five."

"*I* don't know how you convinced your mother to let you come to Chloe's today," Carolyn said.

"I thought you were under some sort of house arrest," Marilyn added.

"I think Mum just got sick of always having me around," Sam said. "I was whining about it so much that it got to be as much of a punishment for her as it was for me. So she's letting me out a bit."

"I'm just glad you're here to help us get through all of these videos," I said. "You really have a good ear for music."

"I told you," Felicia added. "You should hear her sing. Remember when I caught you singing along with those songs on your MP3 player, Sam?"

Sam blushed until her cheeks were the same color pink as the streak in her hair. "That was nothing. I was just mucking around a bit."

"Yeah, but you sounded so great," Felicia told her.

"You are musical," Josh agreed. "I can tell by the comments you're making about the videos."

"Yeah. You know more about music than most people," I agreed. "More than me for sure."

Chloe eyed Sam cautiously for a moment. I got a little worried. Sometimes Chloe can get a little mean when she's jealous, and Sam's singing talent was dipping into her space a little bit. But then Chloe smiled. "Since you know so much about music, how about joining me as one of the three on-air judges for the finals on Friday?" she asked her.

"I thought the audience members were judging the contest," Liza pointed out.

"They are," Chloe said. "But I was thinking we should have three expert judges to comment on each of the singers' performances. Naturally, since I'm the singer on our show, I'm going to be a judge. And Sam should be one, too."

"Well, I guess I can do that," Sam agreed.

Just then Bingo began to howl. "Sorry, Bingo," Chloe giggled. "We need a human judge for this contest."

"I'll do it."

Everyone became quiet at the sound of my voice. To be honest, I was surprised by it as well. Being a judge on a webcast isn't the kind of thing I usually do. But I guess Addie's suggestion that my friends didn't want me on the webcast had made me do it. I wanted to prove to her – and to myself – that my friends did respect me enough to let me have more airtime.

"You?" Chloe asked. "But you said yourself that you don't know a lot about music."

"I know what I like," I said. Then I smiled at Felicia. "Right, Leesh? Just like we were talking about on the phone this weekend."

"Do you really think you can criticize people, Jenny?" Felicia asked me. "I mean, we also decided you were really, really nice."

"Maybe we *need* a nice judge," I said. "I mean, if the five finalists are brave enough to get up and sing on a webcast, shouldn't somebody be here to encourage and congratulate them?"

"That's actually a really good idea," Marc complimented me. "You would represent what the nice people in the audience are thinking."

Chloe nodded in agreement. "What you say could balance out any more detailed criticisms Sam and I might make."

"By detailed, do you mean nasty?" Josh asked.

Chloe giggled. "I like to think of it as *constructive*," she said.

Chapter
TEN

WHILE OUR JUDGES may have been trying to be constructive with their criticism, the Pops were definitely not. In fact, they were downright mean.

"Can you believe how many entries we got for our contest?" I heard Claire say to Sabrina and Maya as Felicia and I walked through the parking lot on Tuesday morning. Actually I think everybody out there must have heard Claire, since she was talking really loudly.

"It's amazing how many fashion victims there are in this school," Sabrina agreed. "It's pathetic."

"I wasn't surprised," Maya said, adding her own venom to the conversation. "You see a lot of hideous outfits around here every day."

"I know," Claire replied. "That's why it's so hard. How do we pick just one person to make over?"

"How do we pick which Pop most needs a personality makeover?" Felicia murmured to me. "They're all so awful, it's hard to decide."

Before I could answer, Chloe came running over to us. She had a huge grin on her face. "I e-mailed the five finalists last night, and gave them a list of karaoke songs to choose from," she said. "They were all so excited! This is going to be huge."

"Huger than huge!" I agreed. It's easy to get caught up in Chloe's enthusiasm.

"I want to make sure we get more viewers than the Pops," Felicia said. "I'd love to show them up!"

That was exactly how we all felt. Nothing would make us happier than to be more popular than the Pops — even if it was only in cyberspace.

But the Pops weren't going down without a fight. A few minutes later, as Sam, Chloe, and I were getting settled into our desks in English class, Dana and Addie walked into the room. They were both wearing bright pink T-shirts. Written on the front of the shirts were the words *STYLE DOCTOR*. On the back they read, *School Style: Thursday Night.*

I had a feeling that if they were both wearing the same shirt, the other Pops were as well. And I had to admit, it was pretty smart of them to advertise their show. My friends, however, were far more critical.

Sam rolled her eyes. "Blimey!" she groaned. "Style doctor? I didn't know you needed a medical degree to put on eye shadow and lip gloss."

"I can't believe they make fun of my T-shirts," Chloe croaked. "Those are the dumbest ones I've ever seen."

Chloe was right. The T-shirt she was wearing today said, *I Wish Every Day Was Friday!* It was a lot cooler than the Pops' pink shirts.

"We're just going to have to advertise our show, too," Chloe said. "But not with T-shirts. That's too easy. We're going to have to do something bigger and better than that."

"Like what?" I asked her.

Chloe shrugged. "I'm not sure. But I'll come up with something that will definitely blow them all away!"

I wasn't sure what Chloe was going to come up with to keep the Pops from landing on top once again, but I couldn't think about it all day long. After all, I had a Spanish quiz to worry about and a math problem that was so hard I needed Josh to help me through it at lunch. Doing the webcast was a lot of fun and all, but I knew my parents wouldn't let me keep doing it if my grades began to fall. Besides, I didn't want my grades to fall. I do pretty well in school, and I'm proud of that.

I also had a student council meeting after school. I braced myself for that one — after all, I'd be sitting in the same room as Addie and her pink T-shirt again. Even though I didn't know exactly what mean thing she would say to me, I knew she'd say something. Like Chloe, Addie will do or say anything when she's feeling competitive. Which, in Addie's case, is pretty much all the time.

But when I walked into the room, it was Sandee, not Addie, who seemed upset with me.

"Jenny, you didn't announce any of our school events on your last webcast," Sandee pointed out.

"I'm sorry," I said. "But with the announcement of the big singing contest, and everything —"

"That's no excuse," Addie butted in. She smiled at Sandee, just to show she was on her side. "You said you would be announcing school events and you didn't."

I glared at Addie. "Neither did you. At least I announced something the first week. You guys don't talk about anything but yourselves. And you're not that interesting."

There was an audible gasp in the room. That had been a pretty intense slam – something I'm not particularly known for. But Addie was really getting on my nerves.

"A lot of people disagree with you on that," Addie retorted. "We have at least fifty people who have entered our makeover contest."

"Only fifty? We have a lot more videos than that."

"You do?" Kia Samson asked me. "Have you seen Jason Winter's?"

I knew why Kia was asking. Jason was her boyfriend, and Kia thought he was wonderful at everything. Unfortunately, he wasn't a good singer. He hadn't even made it through the first cut. But I couldn't tell her that.

"Someone else got to view his video. I heard he was really good," I said. I figured a little white lie couldn't hurt. "But we could only pick five finalists. I'm sure he was really close, though."

Kia frowned slightly. "He had to be. He's got a great voice."

"Who are the finalists?" John Benson asked.

"I can't tell you," I explained. "Chloe has contacted the five finalists, but they've been sworn to secrecy. That way everything about Friday night's webcast will be a complete surprise."

"Well, not everything," Addie said snidely. "No one will be surprised when your show has fewer viewers than ours. Everyone will be logging on to see the magical transformation we're going to make on our lucky prize winner." Addie looked around at all of us. "And because we in student council work so closely together, I'm going to let you in on a secret about Thursday night."

Everyone focused on Addie. Addie smiled back, basking in the glow. She took a deep breath, as though she was about to unearth some hidden information about national security. "I'm going to loan the winner one of my favorite skirts! The green one with the polka dots. She's going to look terrific!"

I sat there for a minute just staring at Addie. Could she really be thinking that was interesting to anyone? I wondered when Addie had become so shallow. And I was sure everyone else in the room was thinking that, too.

But I was wrong. Sandee and Kia were certainly intrigued.

"Oooh. That means the girl you guys chose to make over is short like you, Addie," Kia guessed.

Addie bristled a bit at being called short, but she quickly recovered. "I'm not short. I'm only smaller than you because I'm a year younger."

"True," Sandee agreed. "So does that mean the girl you chose is a sixth grader?"

Addie smiled mysteriously. "I didn't say that."

"Then she's *not* a sixth grader?" Sandee asked.

"I didn't say that, either," Addie replied.

I looked around the room. The boys were obviously bored out of their skulls. This didn't interest them at all. Makeovers were definitely not a boy thing, which explained why none of the guys who hung around with the Pops were part of *School Style.*

But girls and boys were equally interested in *Webcast Underground.* For a minute I thought about giving a clue about who had made it to the finals of our show, but I stopped myself. I had promised my friends not to tell. And I wasn't going to risk the surprise we'd all been working so hard on just to show Addie how much more interesting our contest was than hers. Besides, there really wasn't anything to prove. I knew our show was better than the Pops' webcast.

I just hoped everyone else knew it, too. I know it sounds a little babyish, but I really wanted our show to be the only one people were talking about on Monday morning.

But for people to talk about our show, they were going to have to watch it. And Chloe was not leaving that up to chance. She'd warned me that she was going to plan something huge, and she wasn't kidding. I discovered that the minute I stepped off the bus in the school parking lot on Wednesday morning.

There was a huge banner taped to the wall of the school building. It read:

WEBCAST UNDERGROUND. . .
WHO WILL BE THE SCHOOL'S
NEW SINGING SENSATION?
Find out Friday night at 8:00 P.M.!

That would have been cool enough, even if that had been all Chloe had done. But it wasn't. She and Sam had come up with something even more amazing. A minute later, the two of them were standing right beneath the sign. They were each wearing microphone headsets – like the kind pop stars use when they're onstage. That was because Chloe and Sam were about to be pop stars – at least for a minute – in our school parking lot.

"*Webcast Underground* this Friday night," they sang. "It's really gonna be out of sight! Five singers fight on stage; see who's the best singer of the modern age. What we're trying to tell you is just this: *Webcast Underground* is the one show you can't miss. Now everybody sing along – with *Webcast Underground* you can't go wrong! *Webcast Underground* – our number one show! *Webcast Underground*, it's the best, you know."

Then Chloe and Sam began to work the crowd. They walked among the people, clapping their hands, and singing the last refrain over and over. "*Webcast*

Underground – our number one show! *Webcast Underground*, it's the best, you know." And before long, everyone in the parking lot was singing along.

Well, almost everyone. The Pops weren't singing the catchy new *Webcast Underground* jingle. (Although I could swear, for a minute there, I saw Dana mouthing the words until Sabrina elbowed her in the side.) In fact, they were obviously annoyed that the attention had been taken away from them.

Chloe and Sam had stolen the Pops' thunder in a huge way. The song they'd written was really catchy – like one of the commercials you hear on TV that sticks in your head and won't go away. I had a feeling that everyone in school was going to be humming the same thing over and over all day long: "*Webcast Underground* – our number one show! *Webcast Underground*, it's the best, you know!"

A few minutes later the first bell rang. I hurried through the crowd and made my way toward Chloe and Sam. I just had to congratulate them on our way to English class. "That was awesome!" I complimented them, after pushing my way through the throngs of people trying to get into the building.

"I think it went well," Chloe said. She was trying to sound modest, but the smile on her face gave it all away. She was extremely proud of herself.

So was Sam. "That was brill!" she exclaimed. "Did you see the look on Addie Wilson's face? She looked like she was about to have a cow!"

I giggled. Have a cow. That phrase matched the expression on Addie's face perfectly.

"When did you guys come up with that?" I asked them.

"Yesterday afternoon," Chloe said. "We hung out at my house and fiddled around with some lyrics and melodies."

"That must have taken all afternoon," I said.

"Not at all," Sam disagreed. "It only took an hour."

"We knew we had a hit the minute Bingo started singing along," Chloe joked.

"Exactly," Sam agreed. "He was barking the rhythm!"

Chloe giggled. "What can I say? I have a talented dog."

"He *is* clever," Sam agreed. "By the way, did you find my green hat in your basement after I left? I think I left it at your house."

Chloe shook her head. "I haven't seen it. But I'll check this afternoon."

As we turned the corner into C wing I hurried over to my locker. I just wanted to drop off my coat before racing to English class. As I hurried down the hall, I could hear a buzzing around me. It was the sound of kids all humming the same song. "*Webcast Underground* – our number one show! *Webcast Underground*, it's the best, you know!"

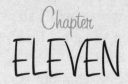

Chapter
ELEVEN

THE POPS WEREN'T GOING DOWN without a fight. By Thursday morning they'd already regrouped and were publicizing their big webcast that evening.

This time they'd made the school parking lot *their* stage. Actually, they'd made it into their runway. The Pops were having a fashion show in the middle of the parking lot!

"Dana is wearing a new pink and white polka-dot miniskirt with a white, short-sleeved blouse. The pink ballet flats tie the outfit together," Addie said as Dana walked across the blacktop in a straight line.

"Claire's wearing the new dark jeans that all the movie stars love, and her red sweater looks great with her hair," Addie continued as Claire took to the runway.

"I don't believe this," Felicia groaned as we walked over to where Rachel and the twins were standing.

Rachel lifted her neck up high and began to walk around in a circle, wiggling her hips back and forth in a really crazy way. "I'm wearing last year's jeans and my cousin's green polo shirt," she said. "Isn't it fancy?"

We all giggled. As usual, Rachel had been able to find

the humor in the situation. When you looked at it from her point of view, the Pops' fashion show was absurd.

Unfortunately, no one but us was looking at it that way. Most people seemed interested in what the Pops were up to. Well, the girls, anyway. The boys didn't care too much about what Claire and Dana were wearing.

"They're going to have a big audience..." Marilyn began.

"... for their webcast," Carolyn said, finishing her sister's thought.

"They've definitely gotten everyone's attention," I agreed. "I wonder who they're going to make over tonight."

My friends all stared at me with surprise. They couldn't believe I'd mentioned any interest in the Pops webcast. But I knew deep down they'd all been wondering the same thing. It was just the way things went in our school. It was impossible not to be curious about the Pops — no matter how hard you tried to fight it.

Which was why I found myself sitting in front of my computer on Thursday evening, waiting for *School Style* to start. I just had to watch, even though I was exhausted from going to my classes and then taking part in the buddy program at the elementary school (it's a program where middle schoolers play games, color, and do crafts with kindergartners). I wanted to see what kind of makeover the Pops could put together. I had a feeling everybody else I knew was doing the same thing.

I didn't have to wait long to find out who had won the Pops' makeover. Less than one minute into the webcast, Claire and Maya introduced a seventh grader named Melissa and began to pick apart everything she was wearing.

I'd seen Melissa around, even though I didn't really know her. She didn't look particularly style-less. She just seemed normal. Like most of us, she wore jeans, shirts, and sneakers most of the time. She had long brown hair that hung straight down her back, and glasses.

The glasses were the first things to go once the Pops got ahold of her. "You don't really need these, do you?"

"Just if I want to see when I'm walking around," Melissa answered.

I giggled. That was actually pretty funny. But the Pops didn't think so. "You should get contacts," Dana told her. "You have pretty eyes."

"My mom said I have to wait until I'm sixteen," Melissa explained.

"You have to convince her," Claire insisted. "It's very important for your new look."

"Well, I don't need glasses when I read," Melissa said. "So I can go without them then, at least."

As Claire and Dana tried to explain how fashion was more important than seeing, Maya was busy twirling Melissa's long brown hair into a French braid. Every now and then, Melissa would wince when Maya pulled too hard.

"Ouch!" Melissa groaned.

"Sometimes beauty is painful," Maya said, trying to sound wise.

As Maya completed the hair part of the makeover, Sabrina began putting makeup on Melissa. "A little eye shadow and blush can go a long way," Sabrina said. "You don't need a lot, or you'll look like a clown." She pulled two hairy black things out of a case. "Have you ever worn false eyelashes?" she asked.

The webcast went on and on. It was thirty minutes of the Pops quoting dumb things they'd read in fashion magazines. Then, finally, Melissa went into another room and put on Addie's skirt and top. And when she came out she looked . . . like a Pop! She really did. I hated to admit it, but they'd changed Melissa from a normal kid into one of their own.

"And tomorrow, Melissa will be eating lunch at our table!" Addie exclaimed. "Won't that be fun?"

Melissa nodded. "I can't wait!" she exclaimed. I could tell she really meant it. Who wouldn't? Despite the fact that few of us would ever admit it out loud, that was where we all would have wanted to eat lunch if we could.

Well, maybe almost all of us. As soon as *School Style* ended, my cell phone rang. It was Chloe. At least I thought it was. The person on the other end of the phone was laughing so hard it was difficult to tell.

"Sometimes beauty is painful," Chloe said, choking on her own laughter. "I think that was the funniest part."

"You watched?" I asked, surprised.

"Of course. Gotta keep up with the competition," Chloe explained. "But I'm not worried. That was the dumbest thing I've ever seen. Our show is going to be so much better."

I knew our singing contest was a better idea than a makeover contest. But despite Chloe's laughter, I knew the Pops had put together a pretty good transformation. I hoped we'd be able to pull off our show just as well.

The next day at lunch, all eyes were on the Pops. Everyone wanted to watch Melissa's debut at the Pops' table. Would the Pops really let a newcomer into their inner circle — even for one day? Or would they make her sit off to the side?

The Pops were definitely aware they were being watched today. They had smug smiles on their faces as they led Melissa across the cafeteria toward their table. (They really did have to lead her, because Melissa wasn't wearing her glasses.)

I hoped Melissa had been able to see her reflection in the mirror when she'd gotten dressed that morning, because she looked really pretty. She was still wearing Addie's clothes. Sabrina had done her makeup again, and I had to admit, those false eyelashes made her eyes look huge.

Melissa sat down at the Pops' table, right between

Addie and Dana. She looked a little uncomfortable, especially since no one at the table was actually talking to her. I guess they figured she'd be gone from their world after today, so why bother spending any more time on her? I felt badly for Melissa. She was being ignored in front of everyone in fifth period lunch.

But Melissa couldn't be ignored for long. All of a sudden I heard her scream. "There's a spider in my soup!" she exclaimed loudly. She leaped onto her chair, petrified. As she jumped up, her arm hit her tray, and her soup spilled all over Addie.

"Look what you did!" Addie shouted.

We all looked. It was impossible not to. What a mess! Addie had been wearing a white blouse. Now it was white and tomato-soup red.

"I'm sorry, but there's a spider . . ." Melissa apologized feebly.

Sabrina looked down at Melissa's tray. Then she picked up Melissa's "spider." "It's your false eyelash," she told Melissa. "It fell off and landed in your soup. Obviously you didn't put it on right."

"I told you this whole makeover thing would be a disaster!" Addie shouted at her friends. "And it was. Just look at my new shirt. I'll never do anything like this ever again!"

While everyone else in the cafeteria was focusing on Addie's shirt, I glanced over at Chloe. She was busy laughing. "I guess that's the end of our competition," she said gleefully.

TWELVE

I WAS GLAD NOT TO have to worry about the Pops competing with our webcast anymore. But I was far from relaxed. By the time Friday evening rolled around, I was actually a nervous wreck. I knew a lot of people would be watching *Webcast Underground*, and not just kids at our school. Chloe and Marc had put posters up all over town advertising our show. That meant lots of people I didn't even know would be watching us.

I wasn't the only one who was stressed out. The five kids who'd been chosen as finalists — Sarah, Emily, Mike, Zach, and Alex — were pretty nervous, too. I think it was finally hitting them that they would be singing live — not just in front of us, but in front of a whole invisible audience.

"I think we should do a run-through of each of your songs," Marc suggested to them. "That way we can work out any problems before we go on the air."

"Great idea!" Chloe exclaimed. She walked over to the laundry folding table that stood next to her basement dryer. "That's funny," she muttered as she bent down and looked around at the floor.

"What's up, Chlo?" Josh asked her.

"My MP3 player's missing," Chloe replied. "I put it on the table earlier and now it's gone."

"Are you sure you put it there today?" Carolyn asked.

"Maybe that's where it was yesterday," Marilyn continued.

Chloe shook her head. "No. I'm absolutely sure it was there. I put it down to play fetch with Bingo for a few minutes. Then the doorbell rang, so I went upstairs to answer the door, and that was the last time I saw it."

"Boy, stuff sure disappears in your house," Felicia pointed out.

"Yeah, like my purple feather pen," I recalled.

"And my sweatshirt," Felicia pointed out. "You never did find that."

"Or my hat," Sam added. "It's like this basement just swallows stuff up."

"Maybe it's haunted down here," Marilyn suggested.

"Yeah, like in that movie," Carolyn agreed. "The one where the dead family tries to get rid of the living family who just moved in and —"

"Stop it!" Chloe shouted. "My house is not haunted!"

We all got very quiet.

"Besides, I can't worry about all your stuff now," Chloe continued. "I've got to find the MP3 player. How are the finalists going to sing without it?"

That made the five finalists very nervous. In fact, we were all nervous. Even Marc. And he hardly ever got stressed out.

"This is bad," he moaned. "We go on the air in half an hour. Chloe, you've got to find that thing soon."

But the MP3 player was gone. We looked everywhere. It had just disappeared.

"What are we going to do now?" Chloe asked. She looked like she was going to cry.

"Don't panic," Sam said. "I can make this work."

"How?" Chloe asked. "I had all their songs downloaded on it. Now they have no accompaniment to sing to."

"I'll call my mum, and she'll bring over my keyboard," Sam said. "I'll play the accompaniment."

"You play piano?" I asked her, surprised.

"For six years," Sam said. "I'm pretty good."

"But I don't have the sheet music for the songs," Chloe said.

"That's okay," Sam said. "I can play by ear. All they have to do is sing the song for me one time, and then I can play it."

"Wow!" I exclaimed. "That's amazing."

"Do you think your mom would drive a keyboard over now?" Marc said. "It's kind of short notice."

"Sure," Sam assured him. "Mum'll do anything to get me to play. We've been fighting about it for weeks. I wanted to stop my lessons, and she had a fit."

So that was what Sam and her mother had been arguing over.

"Well, I'm glad you didn't quit," Marc told her. "Your piano lessons may have just saved our show."

*   *   *

That was no exaggeration. Sam really did save *Webcast Underground.* Just as she'd promised, she was able to play every song the singers performed. She did it so well, it seemed like we'd actually planned to have her accompany them all along. Now I understood why her mom wouldn't want her to give up her piano lessons.

I actually thought Sam was more talented than our five finalists. If it had been up to me, I would have given the prize to her. But I couldn't. We'd promised to give it to one of the kids in the contest.

Luckily it wasn't completely in my hands. Sure I had to give my opinion — I was one of the judges after all. But it was our viewers who would be voting. Thank goodness. I hate to upset people. And no matter which singer I would have chosen as the winner, four other people would have been totally bummed out.

I was able to find something nice to say about each finalist's performance, like the fact that Sarah was able to hit all the high notes in her song without her voice cracking, and Mike was really good at dancing while he sang. Emily kept the rhythm of the song, at least most of the time. Zach had great energy, and Alex amazed me because he knew all the words to a really hard song and didn't mess them up at all.

I was glad I was able to find something nice to say about each of the finalists, because that way Addie would know that my friends weren't ashamed to be around me at all. They respected my opinions. I don't know why I was so concerned with what Addie thought, but I was. Someday I hope to get over that feeling. And I hope it's soon.

The nicest things I had to say, though, were reserved for Sam. We were all seriously impressed with her keyboarding skills.

"I can't believe you want to give that up," Felicia told her.

"You shouldn't stop playing," I agreed. "People would kill to have a talent like yours."

"I know I would," Liza agreed.

Sam blushed lightly at all the praise. "Thanks," she said. "I actually did have fun today."

"Isn't playing the piano always fun?" Chloe asked. "I know singing is."

"That's because you sing the songs you want to, when you want to," Sam pointed out to her.

"Which is all the time," Marc teased.

Chloe turned and stuck her tongue out at him, but she laughed.

"No, seriously," Sam insisted. "I loved playing piano back in England. My teacher, Paul, was really tops. He let me play all kinds of music — classical, jazz, and pop. And we did a lot of improvising. But when we moved to the States, my mum hired this really intense piano instructor. She doesn't let me play any pop music — it's just classical stuff and scales. Lots and lots of scales. It gets so dreary!"

"Maybe you don't have to quit the piano," Josh suggested to her. "Maybe you just have to quit the teacher."

"Josh is right," Felicia agreed. "There are lots of piano teachers out there. Maybe Mr. Sabatino can recommend someone who'll make your piano lessons more fun."

That was actually a good idea. Mr. Sabatino was the music teacher at school. He made music class a lot of fun, even for people like me who can't really sing all that well.

"I suppose it's worth asking him," Sam agreed. "I do love to play. Especially at events like we had today. I guess I don't want to give up piano after all."

"Maybe on the next webcast, you can play piano while I sing," Chloe suggested.

"I thought the winner was going to sing on next week's webcast," Liza pointed out.

"Well, that won't fill a whole show," Chloe said.

"That's true," Marc said. He pulled out his notebook and a pen. "In fact, while we're all here, why don't we . . ." he began.

But before he could even finish his sentence, Bingo came flying down the stairs at top speed. He was barking and jumping around. I guess he was happy to be allowed back downstairs.

"Aruff!" Bingo barked. Then he leaped up, grabbed Marc's notebook in his teeth, and took off like a flash.

"Hey! Give me that!" Marc shouted. He ran off after Bingo. "I need my notebook."

But Bingo didn't stop — not until he'd crawled between the washer and the dryer. It didn't seem like a big enough space for Bingo to fit, but somehow he managed to wedge himself between the two machines. He also managed to wiggle his way out — but only after dropping the notebook. It was actually kind of amazing to see. Only animals can maneuver their bodies that way. No human could have ever pulled it off.

"Oh, great," Marc groaned.

"I'll get it," Chloe said. She reached her arm between the two machines and fished around for Marc's notebook. "Hey, this is weird," she said.

"What is?" Marc asked her.

"There's a whole bunch of stuff stuck back here," Chloe said. She pulled out a gray cloth from between the washer and dryer and held it up. The cloth was actually a gray sweatshirt that said *Joyce Kilmer Middle School Basketball* on the front.

"Hey! That's mine!" Felicia shouted.

Chloe handed it to her. "It's kind of dusty," she told Felicia. "You want me to wash it?"

Felicia shook her head. "I'll wash it at home. I don't want to risk it getting lost again."

Chloe reached back between the machines and pulled out Marc's notebook and her MP3 player. "So that's where it went."

"That must be Bingo's special place," I said. "He's been grabbing our things and sticking them back there."

Chloe gave me a dirty look. "Are you saying my dog's a thief?" she demanded.

I shook my head. "I don't think dogs think of it as stealing. I think he just thought he was playing with new toys."

Chloe reached between the machines again and pulled out more missing items. "New toys like your purple feather pen, Sam's hat, and . . ." Chloe stopped for a minute and reached way in the back. "Hey! Bingo! You took my new green sneaker. I've been looking for that for days. Mom was about to punish me big time for being careless with my things."

Bingo began to jump up and down, happily wagging his tail. He obviously had no idea what Chloe was saying. The only word he'd understood was his name.

"You're gonna have to train him not to take your stuff, Chloe," I pointed out, as I tested my purple pen on my hand to make sure it still wrote.

"I guess so," Chloe admitted. "I'll have to go back and look at the dog training book I bought to see how to do that."

"Maybe you'd better check behind the dryer to make sure Bingo hasn't hidden *that* book, too," Rachel joked.

We all laughed at that.

"Aachoooo!"

Suddenly we heard a loud sneeze. We all turned around and stared at Marilyn. Her eyes were all glassy, and her face looked really pale.

"Gesundheit," Liza said.

"Danks," Marilyn said. "Aachoo!"

"Are you okay?" Sam asked her.

Marilyn shook her head. "I don't feel so great. Is it suddenly freezing in here?"

Carolyn sighed. "Oh, boy. You've got the chills. That's a sure sign. You have the same flu I had."

"I hope not," Marilyn said. "Aaachooo!"

"You'd better go home," Josh suggested. "Otherwise you'll be too sick to be on next Friday's webcast, when we announce the winner."

"Aaaachooo!" Marilyn replied.

"I wouldn't count on her for next week," Chloe said. "Carolyn was sick for more than a week, remember? And this sure seems like the same kind of thing."

Carolyn glanced at her sister. Then a look of fear came over her — the same look that Marilyn had when Carolyn was home sick.

"Don't worry," Liza said, wrapping an arm around Carolyn.

"Yeah," Chloe added. "We'll find something for you to do on next week's show all by yourself. Is there anything you've ever wanted to try?"

Carolyn cocked her head slightly and thought about that. "Well, I *have* always wanted to try doing a trapeze act . . ."

I thought about that for a minute. You can't really do a trapeze act by yourself. You need someone to catch you.

Come to think of it, my friends and I would probably be pretty good trapeze partners. We're pretty good at catching one another when we fall.

Okay, not when we *really* fall. I mean, we're good at supporting each other when we need to. Which was why, even though Chloe's ceilings were too low and too weak to support a trapeze, I was sure we would be able to find something Carolyn could do on her own on our next webcast. With our help, she'd survive a week without her sister by her side. Surviving middle school – no matter what troubles come our way – is what my friends and I do best!

Do Your Friendships Make You Happy?

Do you have so many friends you can barely keep track of them? Or are you the kind of girl who has one or two BFFs who you are incredibly close to? The truth is, it doesn't matter how many friends you have, as long as your friendships make you happy. So are your friendships a source of joy, or are they a pain? To find out, answer these true or false questions.

1. **I smile the most when I am with my friends.**

    True
    False

2. **One of my favorite things to do is spend time with my friends.**

    True
    False

3. I know all of my friends' parents and siblings.

    True

    False

4. I hardly ever fight with my friends.

    True

    False

5. When I get good news, the first person I call is my BFF. We have to celebrate!

    True

    False

6. If I get a message from a friend, I can't wait to call her back.

    True

    False

7. My most cherished possession is something my BFF gave me.

    True

    False

8. I can name all of my friends' favorite foods, colors, and TV shows.

    True

    False

What do your answers say about you?

Mostly true: Smile, you lucky girl! Of course you don't need to be told to smile, you do that all on your own because your friendships keep you happy. It seems you've found the perfect pals for your personality. Congrats!

Mostly false: Uh-oh. You may have gotten yourself into the wrong group of friends. It's not that there's anything wrong with the kids you've been hanging with lately, it's just that you may not have as much in common with them as you might like. Why not try joining a club you find interesting or signing up for a sport you've always wanted to try? Those are two great ways to meet new people and develop friendships with people who have similar interests.

Equal number of true and false answers: You're very lucky to have friends who make you happy at least half of the time. If you want to improve your happiness quotient, though, keep this old saying in mind: Make new friends, but keep the old, one is silver and the other's gold.

Take a sneak peek at the next book!

"We're supposed to have really clear weather tonight and tomorrow," Josh said. He turned slightly so that he was facing Felicia, who was sitting next to him, and Sam and me, who were sitting just behind him. "That's great, because we'll be able to see both the Big Dipper and the Little Dipper through the giant telescope they have at camp."

"I didn't know you were so into astronomy," Sam said.

"Josh is into all kinds of science," Felicia said proudly. "He reads science books just for fun."

I grinned. Felicia was so proud of her boyfriend. Just being around him made her happy.

But there were some people on the bus who were definitely less impressed with Josh's love of all things scientific. Addie and Dana were sitting two rows in front of Josh. They'd heard everything he'd said. "Thanks for the lecture, Mr. Science Geek," Dana remarked drolly.

Addie began to laugh. "Mr. Science Geek, that's a good one." She chuckled.

Dana smiled proudly and laughed even harder.

Personally, I thought Mr. Science Geek was actually a stupid name to call someone, but judging from the way Addie and Dana were laughing, I had a feeling I'd be hearing the same joke all week long. Once the Pops found someone to pick on, they stuck with it. I'd been their victim plenty of times. I guess that's because Addie hates me about as much now as she used to like me back when we were BFFs in elementary school. And she'll stop at nothing to embarrass me. Josh was actually getting off pretty easy. Being called Mr. Science Geek for a week wasn't all that awful. Besides, Josh didn't seem to mind. He'd ignored Dana's comments, and he was still telling the rest of us all about constellations.

Once Addie and Dana realized that their jokes weren't getting under Josh's skin, they stopped laughing and went back to ignoring him. They pulled their makeup bags from their backpacks and started putting on eye shadow.

"I don't know why they're putting on eye makeup," I whispered to Sam. "It's camp. No one wears makeup at camp!"

"Maybe they just want to fit in," Sam said.

"Fit in?" I asked. "With who?"

"With the raccoons," Sam told me. "Did you ever notice how all that mascara and eyeliner makes Dana look like a raccoon?"

That really made me laugh — especially because it was so true! I leaned back in my seat and stared out the window. Already the view had changed. We weren't passing any shopping malls or car dealerships on the road, like we had been when we were closer to home. Now all I could see for miles were trees and a couple of billboards. Then something else caught my eye.

"Hey, guys," I said. "That sign we just passed said CAMP EINSTEIN, NEXT EXIT. We're almost there!"

Will Jenny survive middle school?
Read these books to find out!

#1 Can You Get an F in Lunch?
Jenny's best friend Addie dumps her on the first day of middle school.

#2 Madame President
Jenny and Addie both run for class president. Who will win?

#3 I Heard a Rumor
The school gossip columnist is revealing everyone's secrets!

#4 The New Girl
There's a new girl in school! Will she be a Pop or not?

#5 Cheat Sheet
Could one of Jenny's friends
be a cheater?

#6 P.S. I Really Like You
Jenny has a secret admirer!
Who could it be?

#7 Who's Got Spirit?
It's Spirit Week!
Who has the most school pride —
Jenny's friends, or the Pops?

#8 It's All Downhill From Here
Jenny has to spend her snow day
with her ex-BFF Addie!

Log on to my favorite website!
www.middleschoolsurvival.com

You'll find:
- Cool Polls and Quizzes
- Tips and Advice
- Message Boards
- And Everything Else You Need to Survive Middle School!